GHOST STORIES

Compilation of Real Horrifying-

Demon Encounters

HANNAH J. TIDY

TABLE OF CONTENTS

INTRODUCTION

We live in a world often very dark and sinister, and this is difficult to deny even for the most optimistic and light-hearted ones among us. It is a world teeming with all manner of horror and there is never a shortage of things that can frighten us. Some of us are terrified of things that are very tangible and perceivable through our five senses, others are unsettled by abstract or personal issues, and the few fearless ones appear to fear nothing at all. However, no matter how comfortable we may feel, the vast majority of us share one universal fear, and that is the murky and inexplicable unknown.

That which we can barely even perceive, let alone understand, can be more horrific than a pack of wolves, a deranged killer, or anything else that society and the wilderness have to offer. These are the things that are in the realms of the paranormal, and no matter how many folks experience their own encounter with this underbelly of our reality, the answers and explanations remain ever elusive.

While many people who had their run-ins with the paranormal have found themselves in those situations by chance, for others that isn't quite the case. Despite how horrific we find the idea of possession, ghosts, demons, and hauntings, many of us still retain a sort of morbid, perhaps dangerous, curiosity about the matter. Against better judgment, some folks like to purposely challenge the unknown through mediums such as the infamous Ouija board in the hope of seeing for themselves what might lie on the other side.

Many people dismiss Ouija boards and other, similar matters as mere games that could never hurt anybody and more often than not they are right. But individuals who challenge the demons sometimes find themselves in horrific, even life-threatening, situations that leave the rest of us shaking our heads in disbelief. And although we should always maintain a healthy dose of skepticism, some stories are convincing, as you will find in this book.

You should never play with what you can't understand, and some tales we are about to tell will hopefully make you heed that warning and stay away from things like Ouija boards. The stories found should hopefully satisfy your curiosity on what might happen and dissuade you from learning from your own mistakes.

There is also the matter of those who never asked for trouble and yet suffered paranormal consequences all the same. It appears that some individuals are swamped by demons for no particular reason, turning their lives into an ordeal overnight. We will cover a couple of such stories too.

On a final note, before we begin, it's also worth pointing out that in the circles of paranormal experts and investigators, demons have a fairly clear definition. These evil haunters differ from mere ghosts, evil spirits, poltergeists or the Devil himself. Evil spirits that haunt people, for instance, are generally considered ghosts of those who have passed, while poltergeists are projections of a living person's psyche, usually brought on by negative energy and tremendous inner turmoil. Demons are something else entirely.

These aren't remnants of passed-away loved ones or an enemy; these are forces that are believed to come directly from hellish realms – evil forces too. It is believed that demons have an actual capacity to harm or even kill people, with one of their main objectives being to possess the body of a living human. Cases of possession have traditionally been associated with demons, and it's believed that the only hope that the poor, afflicted souls have is an exorcism.

The very *nature* of demons should be more than enough to show you just how dangerous Ouija boards and similar channels into the beyond can be, but nothing quite compares to first-hand and witness accounts of when disaster strikes.

CHAPTER ONE:
THE ORDEAL OF ROLAND DOE

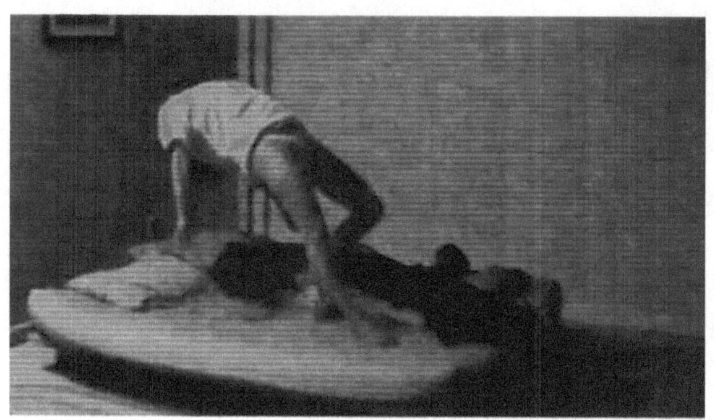

One of the most famous and horrifying stories to ever involve an Ouija board was the horrific tale of an anonymous boy in the 1940s, who was assigned the pseudonym of Roland Doe to protect his identity after the terrible episode that befell him. You may not have heard of Roland, but you are bound to have heard about the 1973s famed horror flick, "The Exorcist." This infamous and successful movie that has been terrifying horror fans for generations was based on a novel of the same name, which was inspired by this very case.

The story of Roland's demonic possession and later exorcism was witnessed and told by as many as a few dozen witnesses and through the diary of one of the involved priests, Father Raymond J. Bishop.

Roland Doe or Robbie Mannheim, which was another pseudonym given to the boy, was just reaching his teen years in the late '40s. He was born to a rather religious family as an only child, and they lived in Cottage City, Maryland when the incidents took off. As the sole offspring and a fairly lonely child, Roland became attached to his aunt. He spent a lot of time with her and she was a rather strong influence on the boy. Among other things, Roland's aunt was said to be involved in all manner of spiritualism, including the use of Ouija boards and other forms of communication with the other side.

This is how Roland himself was first introduced to the board and learned how to use it on his own. The unfortunate discovery of this dangerous tool was to play a major part in Roland's subsequent demonic ordeal, which is believed to have started shortly after his aunt passed away in St. Louis, in 1949. By all indications, the grief-stricken boy had attempted to contact his late aunt through the board, and things took a turn for the sinister.

Roland's family experienced a myriad of peculiarities around the home, seemingly somehow always happening around Roland or when he would enter the room. At first, his parents would just hear strange noises emitting from different areas around their home at night, such as unexplained footsteps. But things became even more clearly unsettling when, as they reported, furniture and various other household objects and appliances inexplicably changed position or moved before their very eyes. Sometimes, certain items would even levitate or be hurled across the room by an invisible force. Roland himself exhibited very unusual behavior and mysterious marks and scratches would appear on different parts of his body. According to other witnesses that later came out, the paranormal phenomena would follow Roland around when he was outside the house too. Strange activity involving inanimate objects in Roland's vicinity disturbed students at his school on at least one occasion.

For those who are well-versed in the paranormal, this would be an important piece of information if true. That's because it eliminates the possibility of a traditional haunting by a poltergeist or a ghost tied specifically to a building. It seemed like the darkness that followed Roland was focused exclusively on him, leading his parents to believe that his Ouija board might have paved the way for a demon to come through and possess the boy's body.

Soon thereafter, the parents sought help from their local pastor. Roland was also evaluated by psychiatrists at Georgetown University Hospital, where he was found to be of sound and healthy mind. The family's pastor recommended to the parents to let the boy spend a night at his house, where he could evaluate what was going on with Roland. Surely enough, the pastor confirmed most of the paranormal activity that his parents described earlier, and he recommended that Roland be brought to Catholic priests for an exorcism.

The first major attempt at an exorcism was conducted at Georgetown by Edward Hughes, who was a Catholic priest himself. The ritual ended in failure when, according to some sources, Roland became uncontrollable, tore a spring off his bed, and inflicted an injury on the priest's arm. This was despite the boy being restrained and tied down to the bed with straps. He had garnered inhuman strength, letting him break one of his arms free from the constraints and attack.

Feeling outmatched, Hughes ceased the exorcisms and recommended that the family find a more experienced and capable exorcist for the task. Roland's parents reported that, soon thereafter, more marks appeared on the boy's body, including the words "St. Louis." The family took this as a message and immediately traveled to a relative's house in St. Louis, Missouri to seek further help for their son.

This was where another priest, Raymond Bishop, was soon contacted. He got in touch with one of his peers, William Bowdern from College Church, and the two went to visit Roland together and start their own investigation into the matter.

The duo of exorcists corroborated the vast majority of previous accounts of Roland's erratic behavior, including the effect he had on objects around him, his aggressiveness, strength, demonic voice and his disgust with anything deemed holy or Christian. This first visit by the priests was also aimed at collecting evidence and removing any doubt before going to their archbishop for permission to conduct a real, major exorcism on Roland. The permission was obtained, the exorcism officially sanctioned by the church, and the real struggle for Roland was now beginning.

The first of the numerous exorcism rituals that would occur over the next two months was conducted at another hospital in St. Louis and in the home of the boy's relatives. As the horrible process went on, several other priests, mainly Jesuits, got involved with the exorcism, including Walter Halloran. With Halloran's assistance, Bowdern conducted the exorcisms with numerous witnesses and with Raymond Bishop keeping logs. It was later also revealed that another man from the hospital's psychiatrist staff kept his own records of the rituals.

These records and the numerous witnesses, especially Halloran, later explained the ordeal. Roland's behavior and struggle were much like what millions of people saw in the 1973s movie. The boy shouted profanities at the priests in an inhuman voice, taunted them, threw dangerous tantrums and the force that appeared to have taken hold of him did everything in its power to derail the exorcism. Particularly disturbing were Halloran's accounts of the bed shaking uncontrollably and unnaturally, Roland speaking in Latin and the inexplicable appearance of ominous marks and words on his body, such as "evil." In a culmination of the struggle, Roland even broke Halloran's nose and drew blood. The exorcists persisted, though, ultimately undertaking up to thirty rituals with the boy.

It appeared as though the exorcists had triumphed and the boy was liberated from his demonic captor. Some witnesses at the hospital said that after the boy screeched one last time and collapsed back on the bed, a foul, sulfuric odor permeated the room.

Although Roland Doe never came forward after the fact to publicly reflect on his experience, it was said by those involved, including Halloran that Roland lived a regular, healthy life in his adulthood. There is no conclusive evidence on what became of the boy, but a few sources offer somewhat varying stories, one of which was that Roland worked for the government and raise a family, having no recollection of his possession. His parents were also rarely in the spotlight and didn't offer many details.

This left a lot of room to speculation during and after the incident, which led to some discrepancies between various media reports and a fair bit of confusion about the details of the story. Something terrible happened to thirteen-year-old Roland, and some will argue that it was an episode of mental illness rather than a demonic possession, but we have no way of knowing for sure. All we can do is hope that the boy got better and that we never discover for ourselves what came come of inadequate and irresponsible handling of an Ouija board.

Before you go on to the next story please do me a favor and tell me what you think of this chapter by leaving a review, visit https://goo.gl/ohTVpc, I would appreciate it very much.

CHAPTER TWO:
THE OUIJA BOARD TOLD ME TO KILL

While it is purported by many that the demons that can be summoned through the Ouija board can inflict physical harm unto the ill-prepared adventurers who play the game, it's sometimes the people at play that do the unthinkable. If against all better judgment, one ends up where they use the Ouija board, they should beware of who is at their side during the ritual. There is no telling what manner of supernatural force can be unleashed and how it might affect those who are present.

In fact, there have been numerous gruesome crimes connected to the Ouija board over the years, and one of the more famous and certainly among the most brutal was the story of David McCallum's horrific murder of fifteen-year-old Michael Earridge.

David McCallum was just seventeen at that dark time in December of 1995, and his friend Pierre Antoine was sixteen. As was later revealed, McCallum had been practicing all manner of satanic rituals for a while already, and he had an entire shrine dedicated to Satan in his London apartment. Part of his place of worship was also an Ouija board, which McCallum used to communicate with demons in his attempts to contact the other side. Both the teens were heavily invested in black magic too, with Antoine acting as a sort of apprentice to McCallum.

On December 2 of 1995, McCallum and Antoine approached Earridge and another fifteen-year-old friend of his on the street and lured them to McCallum's apartment to purportedly watch videos and hang out. Earridge and his friend, Stephen Curran, accepted the invitation and followed the two other teens soon thereafter. Some sources state that all four boys were neighbors who knew each other fairly well before the fact. Whatever their relationship might have been, though, nothing could have prepared the boys for what was in store for them in McCallum's residence.

They immediately found that McCallum's entire room had effectively been turned into a place of Satan worship, which Curran later described as very frightening. Posters, pentagrams, graphic images, satanic song lyrics, Satan-inspired items and ornaments, and much else abounded in the teen's room. The boys also noticed that McCallum was likely a great admirer of Charles Manson, as evident by his collection of magazines and books about the infamous cult leader and convicted killer.

McCallum also had a makeshift and decorated altar that appeared to be dedicated to communicating with demons and the Devil, evident by the boy's Ouija board, candles, black cloth and other symbolism on the altar.

Soon enough, McCallum initiated an Ouija session and used his board to summon the Devil. He asked if Satan was present and what he wanted him to do. Things turned violent when Antoine took Earridge's hand and put it on the glass that McCallum was using on the Ouija board, telling him he would slice his finger off if he refused to participate in the ritual. Now terrified and unwilling to stay, Michael cooperated against his will.

This was when the Ouija board reportedly spelled out the word "kill" and Michael decided that he had enough and would go home. Antoine stopped him, however, telling him that his departure before the ritual was complete was against his master's desires and that he wasn't going anywhere. Antoine then hit the boy on his head to stun him.

The whole ordeal escalated to madness when McCallum took a long, terrifying combat knife, pushed Michael on the bead, and stabbed him in his neck and chest area, inflicting lethal injuries upon his victim. Petrified by this deranged assault, Curran was paralyzed by fear and didn't know what to do. McCallum stopped stabbing Earridge only when Antoine told him to calm down as the boy was dead now. Unfazed and satisfied, McCallum complied and collected himself, as his perceived sacrifice to the Devil was now complete.

Fortunately, the two Satanists did not attack Curran. Instead, they made him handle the blade and leave fingerprints, threatening to frame him for the grotesque crime they had just committed if he ever dared to break his silence. McCallum and Antoine put little effort into disposing of the body. They just wrapped Michael's corpse up in sheets and moved him to another floor of the same building.

Curran was allowed to leave shortly after the incident, but the threats that the teens made against him did not work. Soon thereafter, he told McCallum's father about everything that happened, and the police were quickly on to David and he was arrested that very night. During his apprehension, McCallum reportedly couldn't stop smiling and he never once tried to deny his horrendous crime. But he brought into question the degree of his personal responsibility for the murder, rather choosing to plea to manslaughter instead of murder.

On the surface, his defense was simple because he alleged that the demons made him do it, but he went into more detail on everything. McCallum said that he was no stranger to making sacrifices as he had done the same to numerous animals, all because of Satan and the demons that talked to him through the Ouija board. He further argued that his hand was guided by the Ouija demons to commit the crime and that he couldn't be blamed. He pinned all of the responsibility on what he referred to as "demon madness." McCallum said that the demons spoke to him in a voice in his head, which commanded him not only to kill Michael but also to buy his deadly knife before the fact. Michael was also the first and last human that McCallum sacrificed to his perceived overlord.

McCallum also persisted in his deranged attitude toward the whole ordeal, constantly smiling and grinning throughout the questioning and the later court proceedings, maintaining that the voice said to kill. A psychiatrist was involved and, after evaluating the teen, he concluded that he was suffering from a rather serious case of schizophrenia, earning McCallum his manslaughter plea. Instead of prison, he was committed to a mental hospital, where he remains.

Although a psychiatric evaluation is solid proof to the contrary, many still believe that a higher, dark force was at play and had taken possession of the boy. McCallum was also said to have had history with mental problems prior to the murder itself. Another point of some contention among psychiatrists and other interested parties was the effect that the Ouija board might have had on McCallum's sanity. There are those who say that the board pushed his schizophrenia to new, dangerous heights, whether or not he summoned demons.

One thing is for certain, however, and it is that whether human or supernatural, a demon was definitely at work on that bloody day that left Michael Earridge dead.

CHAPTER THREE:

THE CARROLL FAMILY CALAMITY

Another case of apparent madness with an Ouija board at the epicenter of events occurred much more recently, on Christmas Eve of 2014. Following the usage of an Ouija board, a British family from Consett, County Durham went through a string of horrific tribulations that seemed to continuously escalate from bad to worse.

The story unfolded with Paul Carroll, who attempted to establish contact with the dead through the board on that day. After the ritual, Paul believed that evil spirits got through from the other side and take possession of Molly, a family dog. This belief caused an outburst of paranoia in Paul, who then committed a despicable act of cruelty against his pet. He drowned the dog in a bathtub, dismembered its carcass, and attempted to hide the evidence by shoving the remains into a nearby drain.

After the dog's mangled corpse was removed from the clogged drain by service personnel and neighbors caught wind of what he had done, Paul was reported to the police and promptly apprehended. At first, he simply stated that the family pet died during an Ouija board session when it became possessed, not mentioning his own hand in the animal's gruesome fate. Soon thereafter, however, Paul came around and admitted what he did, explaining that he first tried to bury the dog unsuccessfully, which forced him to chop it up into pieces to dispose of the body and remove its microchip.

He maintained that some evil ghosts or demon possessed his dog through the Ouija board and that he had to put it down. But his heinous act had him convicted with a suspended sentence, the rest of his pets taken away, and he was specifically prohibited from owning any other animals.

This was only the beginning, however, as the story reached a bizarre second chapter in early February of 2015, shortly after the incident with the family dog. Despite everything that happened with Paul, the rest of his family continued to use the Ouija board and meddle with the spiritual world. Paul's wife Margaret Carroll and stepdaughter Katrina Livingstone undertook an Ouija session of their own around a week after Paul pled guilty to his animal cruelty charge and while he was still under arrest. Reportedly, the two women tried to contact their deceased dog from the other side.

As one of their neighbors reported, Katrina told her she and her mother used an Ouija board and received a chilling message predicting that they were both going to die. Emergency services were called in the next morning when the entire Carroll home was engulfed in huge flames and an enormous cloud of thick smoke.

Initially, there were abundant speculations going around that the fire was related to some paranormal activity. However, it turned out that the two women were so petrified by the supposed message they received from the Ouija board they committed suicide and escape their grim fate. When the firefighters and emergency medical personnel arrived on the scene, however, they found Katrina and Margaret outside of the house in their backyard. They were hospitalized, but sources said to the press that the reason for their hospitalization was not the fire itself. Nonetheless, they were taken in pending a police investigation. The fire was dangerous due to its size and the gas canisters on the premises, necessitating the evacuation of nearby neighbors. The Carroll home had to be demolished because of the extensive damage.

As the investigation soon showed, the two women agreed to commit suicide together by swallowing a large number of pills and setting fire to their own house. As the flames spread, however, the two changed their minds and quickly vacated the premises, after which they were found by firefighters. They admitted to arson and were tried for their reckless act in court, both receiving four-year sentences.

While it does little to excuse the unscrupulous endangerment of the entire neighborhood, the two still stuck to their claim they received a death threat from the Ouija board. There's no telling what got into the minds of the Carroll family at that dark Christmas time and how much of an influence the

Ouija board might have had, but it's clear these were rather disturbed individuals. The stepdaughter Katrina had a long track record of sorrow of her own where she lost her children, and Margaret had a history of mental issues and involvement with black magic.

Whether these people were already insane or their Ouija board pushed them over the edge, there is no concrete evidence of demonic meddling in their lives despite their claims. All we are left with is a story of catastrophe and cruelty with an Ouija board at the center.

CHAPTER FOUR:

MICHAEL TAYLOR'S POSSESSION

While talk and arguments of insanity and emotional instability are always there with stories of demonic encounters, Ouija boards are not. Sometimes, unfortunate individuals come under a perceived demonic influence without ever meddling with unknown forces from the other side. Such people don't play with Ouija boards or other dark games and they never ask for trouble, but affliction befalls them.

This terrible fate would fall on one Michael Taylor, whose story has since become possibly the UK's most infamous case of alleged possession coupled with horrific murder. The incidents occurred during the 1970s in a small and serene town of Ossett in West Yorkshire. The population numbered less than twenty thousand people who lived in a very peaceful and safe, mostly Christian English community, and nobody could have dreamed that the community would be shaken to its core by such savagery in 1974.

By the vast majority of accounts, Michael Taylor was a mild-mannered and rather amiable member of the community, never getting into trouble with anybody in the town. His life wasn't without its downturns, however, as his longstanding injury brought him recurring pain and difficulties with finding a job. Besides these few hardships, Michael led a fairly normal family life and fathered five children with his wife, Christine. They were known by their neighbors to be a functional, happy family. Michael and his wife were also perceived by the community as not being all that religions despite their environment. While the majority of townspeople regularly attended church, the Taylors visited less frequently.

Things took a turn soon when one of Michael's friends talked him into trying to engage with a local church group. This special group was organized and led by a charismatic and young Marie Robinson, also a preacher at her age of twenty-one. It didn't take long for Michael to develop an interest and start frequenting the group's meetings and other activities.

Over time, he appeared to become more and more devout, with some speculating that his dedication may have been to the girl rather than the faith. The church group held somewhat strange beliefs and performed all sorts of unique rituals, including particular forms of exorcism, which Michael readily attended. Some of Marie's preaching concerned what she described and perceived as the evil power of the Moon. Sometimes, Michael would be away from home all night, and many saw this as inappropriate, especially his wife.

Taylor's home environment also began to change due to shifts in his behavior and overall attitude. It was much unlike him, but Michael neglected his family and expressing a fair bit of negativity toward them. He appeared to be much more prone to frustration and angry outbursts at and away from home. Michael espoused very peculiar convictions, grew increasingly irritable and erratic and showed more and more that he may be obsessed with Marie Robinson.

Needless to say, both the neighbors and his wife started to notice that Michael was changing from the balanced, kind family man that they know to something else. That something else appeared more sinister and unhinged by the day, and Christine grew increasingly suspicious that the church group and especially Marie were a detrimental influence on Michael. Christine suspected that her husband and Marie were engaging in an affair.

Christine would not stand for this long, so she confronted her husband and tested her suspicions. She did this during one of the group's gatherings, in front of everyone. She did that and she openly accused her husband of being unfaithful with Marie, which immediately sparked an incident.

It was as if something foreign to all those who knew him overpowered Michael and sent him into a bout of rage. This outburst of aggression was directed at Marie Robinson herself, however, without even addressing his wife's accusations. Reportedly, other members of the group had to bring Michael under control, as it appeared he was about to assault Marie physically.

Marie later explained that Michael turned into something unrecognizable at that moment and that she was terrified that he might kill her. But she and the entire group let bygones be bygones the next day and they all forgave Michael, who claimed to have absolutely no recollection of the moment he lashed out. None of this was anywhere near the worst that would happen, though, and the bizarre changes in Michael's character appeared to only escalate as time went on.

Soon thereafter, those around him believed that he had somehow come under the influence of one or more demons, and it was agreed upon to conduct an exorcism on October 5 of 1974. The exorcism was to be performed in a local church in the next town of Barnsley by two priests, Peter Vincent and Raymond Smith. The exorcism itself was to be another horrific episode in Michael's life that would go on through the entire night and into the next morning.

As the ministers began their ritual, Michael immediately transcended any notion of normal human behavior. His body would shake and spasm uncontrollably and he got violent. Michael was beside himself, and he cursed and attacked the ministers, trying to scratch and bite them as if he were a wild animal. After a while of struggling to control him, the ministers tied Michael down to continue with the exorcism. Throughout the night, crucifixes were put into his mouth and the priests used copious amounts of holy water on him in the course of the ritual. As the ordeal went on, Michael kept trying to break free and attack his exorcists.

At one point, the priests became convinced that Michael was possessed by forty different demons, representing all manner of human depravity. By morning hours, the priests believed that they had successfully banished the vast majority, while the demons of insanity, murder, and rage were believed to still have a hold over the man. The exorcists were at the end of their wits by this hour, though, which is why they concluded the ritual on the next day.

This reportedly did not sit well with Raymond Smith's wife, however, and she even said that God spoke to her at that moment, warning her that Michael's demon of killing would make him murder his wife, Christine. The priests stuck to their decision, though, and Michael and Christine went home to recuperate for tomorrow's trials.

Just a couple of hours after they got home, the terrible omen became fulfilled when Michael brutally murdered his wife in their home. The killing was all shades of gruesome and atrocious. He first strangled Christine to kill her, after which he mutilated her. The poor woman's eyes were gouged out, her tongue cut out, and most of her face removed or at least horribly disfigured in the savage attack. After inflicting this unspeakable horror upon his wife, Michael killed the family dog in a no less brutal manner, after which he dismembered the body. Luckily, the children were left untouched and Michael promptly left the house.

He went out into the street naked and drenched in blood. He dragged himself around the town, staggering, shouting out loud that the blood on his body was that of Satan. Michael soon ran into the police, which apprehended him on the spot and went to investigate his home, where they faced the sickening crime scene.

The town of Ossett and the country far beyond it were shocked by what had transpired. This demonic slaying caught a lot of attention and sparked a lot of debate about many aspects of the case and later trial. Michael claimed that demonic forces were ruling over him, and he explained that the murder was simply non-existent in his memory, much like the incident at the church. He even believed that his late wife too was taken hold of by an evil outside force.

Lots of blame and lots of theories were thrown around in the public ranging from those who believed Michael was mentally ill, over those who believed he had been indoctrinated, all the way to folks who believed that he was possessed. Peter Vincent, who received a lot of criticism for his exorcism ritual, stuck to his belief that demons were at work. The church group that Michael became heavily invested in was also labeled as being very cult-like in nature, and many people pointed to their peculiar beliefs and rituals, while others cast the blame on the exorcism exclusively.

The majority of people seemed to conclude this was a case of religious fanaticism and paranoia feeding into each other throughout Michael's community, ultimately pushing him over the edge. The killer stuck to his story, though, and he was found not guilty and declared both clinically and legally insane, which landed him in a facility for the criminally insane. His stay at two institutions would last just four years, however, before he was released.

As fate would have it, Michael was apprehended once again as recently as 2005, when he was charged with sexual harassment. Once again, severe punishment eluded him, and Michael spent three years more in treatment and community service. There is little information on what became of him after that.

To this day, this remains one of Britain's most notorious cases of alleged demonic possession and it is still debated. Whether Michael was drawn to kill by cult influence, insanity, or actual demons will remain a mystery locked deep down in his warped mind for the most part. Whatever the cause was, the friendly family man that Michael's community once knew has been gone for decades.

Creepy right! If you like this story or any of the other stories you've read, please let me know by leaving a short review. You can do this by visiting https://goo.gl/ohTVpc and leaving your thoughts. Thank you

CHAPTER FIVE:

THE DEVIL MADE ME DO IT CASE

Such was the public's dubbing of this bizarre case and its trial for the first murder in the history of the small town of Brookfield, Connecticut. Just a few years after the horrific episode of Michael Taylor, America had its own major case of murder involving allegations of a demonic possession in February of 1981. What made this incident unique was that the allegations of a demonic possession didn't come exclusively as the ramblings of a deranged killer on trial for his life. Rather, demonic possession was the official stance and plea of the perpetrator's defense in court.

Arne Cheyenne Johnson, the assailant just nineteen at the time of the murder, had a run-in with perceived demonic forces prior to the fact.

In summer of 1980, his girlfriend Debbie's preteen brother David Glatzel was thought to be possessed by an evil force, and the family sought to have him exorcised. The illustrious paranormal investigators and demonologists Ed and

Lorraine Warren, along with priests, looked into the case and concluded that the young boy was possessed by forty-three demons.

That story began when David told the local priests and his sister a disturbing story of a demonic encounter. He described being visited by a horrific old man with hooves and horns, who came with numerous other figures in frightening costumes. Unlike just a regular nightmare that comes and goes, this experience, whatever it was, seemed to affect David's life a great deal. His whole attitude became much more sullen and uneasy. The encounters persisted, and David also reportedly had unexplained bruises and other injuries appear on his body due to an unknown cause. It was also at this time that Debbie asked Johnson to move into her home to help her brother.

The priests asked for help tried blessing the house and helping in other ways, but their activities seemed to only aggravate the boy's horrible apparition. The Brookfield priests then contacted the diocese in Bridgeport, Connecticut. For the first time in their history, the diocese actually sent in their investigators to look into the case of supposed demonic activity, which also later gave credence to the story in the eyes of the police.

Assisted by the Warrens and numerous priests, multiple exorcisms were performed on David, many of which were attended by Johnson himself. This was when the upcoming events that shook the nation next year were already in the making. It's believed that Johnson started on the path toward trouble during one particular exorcism ritual when he essentially taunted the demons in David. The Warrens and others who were present said that Johnson vocally challenged the demons to take possession of him and that he would fight them head-on. After that, the witnesses explained, Johnson became increasingly aggressive and it was believed that he was possessed himself. David was reportedly getting better in the time that followed.

Soon thereafter, toward the end of the year, Arne Johnson and Debbie rented an apartment of their own, and that was when the victim Alan Bono came into the picture because he was the landlord. Johnson changed, however, behaving in a way that was very unbecoming of him. Friends and family knew Arne as a well-adjusted young man who didn't shy away from work and from helping out his loved ones. He never broke the law and had no criminal record. Debbie later explained that he routinely entered strange states of trance and was prone to problematic behavior.

On that fateful day on February 16, 1981, Johnson and his girlfriend were spending the day with a couple of other siblings and relatives. They were later joined by Alan Bono, who offered to take them out to lunch at a local café. The group went and, as revealed during the court proceedings, there was quite a bit of drinking going on between Alan and Arne, which was confirmed by a waitress who served them wine.

An air of uneasiness and tension slowly permeated the atmosphere when the group found themselves back at the apartment later on and, at some point, Alan was said to have made an inappropriate remark about Debbie. This led to a heated argument between Johnson and Bono, where Johnson reportedly hissed and growled at Bono. The argument escalated exponentially until Alan ended up stabbed by Johnson four times in the stomach. In the days that followed the killing, quite a few people maintained that Johnson was possessed at the time, including the Warrens, Johnson's mother, Debbie, and priests.

After Johnson's arrest, Martin Minnella, a defense lawyer, volunteered to take the case on for free and represent Johnson during the trial. This was when the case gained enormous amounts of attention from the public, as Minnella vowed to prove that Johnson was possessed by at least one demon. Rather than choosing to plea insanity or mental impairment, as is usually done with such cases, the lawyer went with possession explicitly.

Reporters and regular folks flocked in to follow the fascinating demonic murder trial. Minnella intended to use recordings of David's exorcisms and put priests and the

Warrens on the witness stand to corroborate the phenomenon. The lawyer was inspired by similar cases observed in the UK, and he hoped to conduct the first successful defense on grounds of demonic possession in American history.

The plea was not to be, however, as the judge shot down the defense's proposal soon thereafter. While he still maintained his belief that Johnson had been possessed, the lawyer was forced to make a different plea for his client, and this was self-defense.

After a couple days' length of court proceedings, Johnson was convicted of first-degree manslaughter with a minimum sentence of ten to twenty years in prison.

However, his good behavior while incarcerated earned him an early release and incredibly enough he served short of five years of his term. Toward the end of his time in prison, Johnson and Debbie married and raised a family after his release.

While a significant portion of those who followed and commented on the case criticized the Warrens and expressed great skepticism about many aspects of the story, some have remained convinced that Johnson was possessed. His wife Debbie continued to research matters of the paranormal and, years later, she still commented on her husband's case with more conviction. Debbie said that Arne should have never challenged whatever evil had taken hold of her brother, adding that it was a major mistake.

Martin Minnella, who was criticized by some as taking the case on as a personal publicity stunt, also sticks to his beliefs. Years later, he still said that the case changed his life and that many other violent offenders sought his council, hoping that he could reduce or prevent their sentences. Johnson's case was one-of-a-kind for him, though, and he explained that unlike those that came after it, this one was based on facts.

So, what really happened on that bloody day? If the killing was just a result of a drunken feud, what drove that jury to conclude that it was manslaughter rather than murder? It's likely that the uniqueness of this case may have had them at least somewhat convinced of the demonic supposition, but that remains uncertain.

Plenty of other people to this day believe that something supernatural was at play, though. Unlike in many other similar cases, this perpetrator was never deemed insane or unstable, and yet he got off with a light sentence. This gives the claims an aura of authenticity and rightfully earns this case the accolade of being one of the most famous American incidences of murder by demonic possession.

CHAPTER SIX:
GAMES OF HORROR

As you have hopefully established by now, the incomprehensible world of demons and other paranormal phenomena is not to be messed with. Everybody would be well-advised to stay away from any games and activities purported to summon demons, ghosts, spirits of the dead, or any other paranormal force. In accordance with human nature, however, plenty of such games exist despite the potential risks, and the Ouija board is just one of many. Ouija boards are famous, as is Bloody Mary, so most folks have already at least heard of these games in passing. We will look at a couple of dark games that are less renowned but possibly just as dangerous, if not more.

Many paranormal games exist nowadays and the number of purported ways to contact the dead has risen significantly since the internet became more accessible to people throughout the world. Forums and other networks are filled with various methods and games from users told of these practices by others or experimented with and created them on their own. Many of them come and go without stirring up much interest, but every now and then, one of them stirs up a storm.

One such game is called The Three Kings, which apparently originated from Reddit, although some responders claimed that they knew of the game prior to its publication under a different name.

Either way, the original Reddit post detailed the instructions to play an apparently rather spooky game, and the objective and consequence of the ritual were left fairly ambiguous.

The Three Kings is a game played by one main actor and an assistant, ideally someone close and trusted. The game's instructions stress the importance of both these participants being emotionally and spiritually sound individuals with stable lives and of sober minds. Substance abuse in conjunction with the ritual is emphasized as dangerous. When a willing and trusted partner is found, the ritual requires quite a few other things.

It must be undertaken in an empty, quiet room that ideally has no windows. If windows can't be avoided, they should be covered up well with whatever means are available.

Other ingredients include a pack of candles, lighter, one bucket of water, one mug, a fan, two large mirrors, three chairs, an alarm clock, a phone with a full battery charge, and a small and handy object of great sentimental value to the owner. Once all these things have been gathered, the daring person is ready to play the game.

The ritual starts at 11 PM with the organization of the game room. First, one main chair should be placed in the very middle of the room and face northward. This chair will serve as the *throne*. On either side of this chair, the other two should be placed to face it from about an arm's length distance. One of these will serve as the *queen's chair* while the other will be the *fool's chair*.

Then, the two mirrors should be placed on the chairs – one on each – leaning against the backrests of the chairs so it makes the mirrors perpendicular to the seats. The mirrors will face the throne chair and each other and the person seated in the throne should be able to glimpse his or her reflection in each mirror with peripheral vision only. This should be possible so it requires no movement of the head or eyes, allowing the person sitting in the main chair to glimpse the mirrors while keeping their eyes forward.

The bucket and the mug should then be placed in front of the throne chair, close but just out of reach. The electrical fan goes behind the throne and will blow at it from behind at the medium power setting in a continuous, fixed current of air. It's important to turn the fan on and leave it turned on.

Then, the *player* should exit the room and leave the door open, heading to the bedroom.

In the bedroom, the candles, lighter, alarm clock, and phone should be right next to the bed and within reach. To be safe, it's best to put the phone on a charger to ensure a full battery when the time comes. The alarm clock is to be set to 3:30 AM. Then, the individual should turn off the lights and go to sleep.

Once that alarm goes off at 3:30, the main part of the game begins. If you do this for some insane reason, the instructions will be important, even more so than before according to the post. Shut off the alarm and keep the lights off. Have your *power object* with you, take your phone, light up a candle, and head back to the ritual room. It is paramount that the player is seated in the throne chat no later than 3:33.

Now, there are several signs here, called red flags, which are to be looked out for. If any of them are seen, the ritual must immediately be aborted, as it will later be too late. Red flags to look out for are: your phone did not charge; the alarm clock did not go off at the exact time required; the door leading to the ritual room is closed; the fan is turned off; you didn't make it to the chair by 3:33 AM. As the instructions further emphasize, if these signs are seen, it won't be just a matter of ceasing the ritual and going back to bed. Rather, both the principal individual and the partner, and anybody else on the premises, must leave the house immediately and not come back until after 6:00 in the morning.

If everything is as it should be, you can sit on the throne. Remember two more things, however: you are not to look at the mirrors at any point in the ritual and the candle must be kept alight and shielded from the fan. Once seated properly, the principal individual is to focus exclusively on the darkness in front, never once looking at the mirrors or at the candle in their hand.

The poster of the game further explains those who made it to this point may now ask whatever questions they have, and maybe their questions will be answered. If the answers come, they will seem to emanate from the mirrors, one of which is the fool while the other is the queen. It will be up to you to figure out which is which.

The ritual goes on until 4:34 AM and the participating partner should be ready for this. The assistant is to come in and call you by name to wake you up, so to speak, and if you don't respond, they should call your phone. If that doesn't work either, they should use the mug and bucket of water to help bring you back.

The game is designed so it provides two failsafe options to end the game if things go south. Leaving the throne on your own before the designated time is not acceptable. If there is trouble or an unknown force affects you, the fan will blow out the candle if your body is moved. Second, you must cling hard to your sentimental object, which is supposed to keep you *here.*

The original poster was very mysterious about the purpose of a lot of the steps, as you can see, but he was very adamant in stressing the importance of adhering to the instructions perfectly to stay safe. He didn't want to go into what happens during the ritual either. He simply left the instructions and urged people not to try it.

The Three Kings game has since gained a lot of traction online, with hundreds or even thousands of people responding with their results. The stories range in believability and they portray an array of different experiences, many of which are bone-chilling. The accounts are coming in both from those who conducted the ritual successfully and those who messed up the instructions. Some were attacked by their own reflection when looking at the mirror, some fell into deep states of trance, while others lost consciousness and woke up with no memory of what happened. Whatever it is that may be at play with this game, it has been published for a few years now, and many folks took notice all over the world.

All this is just to illustrate a single example of the rituals that can be found online by everyone. Another terrible example is the Triple Mirror Game, which is supposedly a way to detect spirits that may be lurking around your house. The Midnight Man and the Elevator Game are yet another two examples. The rituals to summon the unseen forces of other realms are virtually endless, and thousands, if not millions of people from all over the world guarantee from first-hand experience that these rituals succeed at fulfilling their horrific purpose.

CHAPTER SEVEN:

DON'T PLAY THE ELEVATOR GAME

Where did the Elevator Game come from? It seems to have appeared in Internet forums at some point around 2015, already ingrained as a part of the urban legend subculture. Unlike other trends, the Elevator Game cannot be sourced back to an original point. Some have claimed that because the legend originated in Japan and Korea, the western audience, that it eventually migrated to, would not be able to trace the source back. But the Internet is a vast place, and in recent years has debunked urban legends that lasted for decades. So why should sourcing the Elevator Game be any different? The strange, sudden appearance of the game leads one to believe that it was otherworldly in origin.

Because that is the entire premise of the Elevator Game: a trip to the Otherworld. There is no concrete evidence as to what this Otherworld really is, for it does not hold similarities to any known Land of the Dead in Asian folklore. Instead, the supposed Otherworld that the Elevator Game takes you to is a dark, mirrored reflection of our own world. Everything inside buildings will look the same, but when you look out the window, all you will see is black, an endless stretch of pitch black—except for the burning, neon red cross in the distance. Nobody knows what happens when you walk outside the doors, for nobody has dared to try.

The cross is not a symbol generally located in any Asian mythologies, which again leads one to the conclusion that this game was not based on ay pre-existing stories or folktales. Instead, the strange uniqueness and simplicity again lead one to believe that it comes from true experience.

The minute details of the rules for the game can vary, depending on where you research them from, but the base rules remain the same. They will be listed below, but as to whether you should play this game for yourself or not? Take this story as your warning.

The game must be played in a building, with an elevator, and 10 or more floors. Hotels or apartment buildings are of course your best options. Do not take cameras, phones or other electronics in with you, the game won't work in the presence of such items. Though some rules claim certain times work better than others, there is no set rule saying when you can and cannot play. For most paranormal games and experiences, it is recommended to play at 3:00 AM: the witching hour. Once you have selected your building, start on the first floor. Press buttons to the following floors in this order: 4, 2, 6, 2, 5, 1—at every floor, do not step off. Instead, stay inside and press the next button immediately.

Part of the game includes the woman on the fifth floor. It has been reported by many that play the game that when you reach the fifth floor, a woman may come in the elevator. She is a demon and will do everything in her power to make you talk to her. She may even appear as someone you know. You must not look at her, speak to her, or acknowledge her in any way. In doing so, not only will you fail the game, but the consequences will follow you long after the game has finished.

If you succeed at all the steps and press the final button for the first floor, two things can happen. One—the elevator will take you to the first floor. This means you have either failed to play the game correctly, or the Otherworld has rejected you. In this case, walk out of the elevator and don't look back over your shoulder. Two—the elevator will instead move up to the tenth floor. When you exit on this floor, you will be in the Otherworld. In order to get back to your own dimension, you will have to play the game again, identically.

Since the game went semi-viral among the community of paranormal enthusiasts, there has been a wash of stories from people who played the game, and either succeeded or failed. Writers and vloggers alike have attempted. The following story from a young woman is not, however, a simple recounting of her experience. Instead, it is a warning to everyone: do not play the Elevator Game.

The young woman in question was living in an apartment with her boyfriend, and both were fair paranormal enthusiasts. He was much more involved than she, and one of his current cases that he was stuck on was the tragic death of Elisa Lam. The mysterious death of the traveler found in a hotel water tank has baffled theorists for years, who have never been able to find an explanation—for her death, or for the strange behavior she exhibited the night before, immortalized on security camera. One of the main theories being bounced around is that Elisa Lam was playing the Elevator Game.

When the young woman's boyfriend brought this to her attention, she immediately laughed it off. There were too many inconsistencies with Elisa's story and the rules of the Elevator Game, and besides, the young woman insisted, the entire game was bogus. But her boyfriend did not let it go and continued to bring it up. Finally, the young woman came up with an idea. If she would play the game and prove it wasn't real, he would stop talking about it. While recounting her tale, the woman takes this moment, right when her boyfriend agreed to her idea, as the moment when she knew he didn't believe in the game either. He was a real believer in ghosts and demons, and if he really believed such a dangerous game existed, he would never let her play it. So, armed with no fear and a staunch belief that nothing would happen, the woman started her research. She chose a building in the downtown Atlantic area, one with enough floors to play the game. One evening, she headed into the lobby and began.

At first, the game played out as she expected. The woman pressed the buttons for each floor in the correct order, and nothing out of the ordinary happened. She was ready for the whole game to be over and to head home and prove her boyfriend wrong—until she reached the fifth floor.

The woman admits to her first mistake: she had been watching the light above the doors, and not the button panel, to watch the floors change. So when the doors opened, her eyes automatically turned downward and locked onto a little woman stepping into the elevator—Petite, pretty, with blonde hair.

Instantly, the young woman remembered the rule about the fifth-floor woman. She had already broken the first rule by looking at her. Suddenly quite afraid, she looked staunchly at the button panel and refused to acknowledge the strange woman's presence any further. She pressed the button for the first floor, eager for the game to be over.

The stranger began to talk, claiming that someone on the floor needed medical assistance, and she had come to look for help. Immediately, the young woman knew this was untrue. If someone really did need help, this stranger would have pulled her off the elevator, not get on with her. She pressed her lips together and stared resolutely ahead. At this lack of response, the strange woman started yelling. All sorts of profanities left her mouth, sharp and biting.

The young woman had never been so afraid in her life. She had her hands clenched together into fists, and her entire body was shaking. The elevator seemed to be taking forever just to reach the bottom floor. It was only five levels, how could it possibly stretch on for such an eternity?

The strange woman had stopped yelling. In the ensuing silence, whimpers of tears came out. They started quietly but became almost deafening. The young woman recalls that she couldn't stand to listen to them, that it sounded so hideously pathetic, it made anger boil irrationally in her blood. The crying got louder and louder and louder until the young woman found that she just couldn't take it anymore, and she snapped.

She had never been a woman of violence, but trapped in the elevator, without hesitation, she grabbed the back of the strange woman's head and slammed it into the metal doors. She screamed at the stranger, telling her to shut up.

Unsatisfied, she did this again and again. Blood matted in the front of her blonde hair and trickled down her face. Then the elevator doors dinged open, and she realized with mounting horror what she had done.

The little blonde woman slowly looked up at her. There was no more anger in her expression, only a sick sort of satisfaction. She only smiled, and then she walked off the elevator.

The young woman stared after her. She couldn't believe what she had done. Not only had she acknowledged the fifth-floor woman, breaking the most important rule of the game, she had let a stranger manipulate her so easily. Eager to get out, the woman stepped forward. The elevator chimed, and the doors slid shut. Without a single button being pressed, the elevator began to ascend.

The woman freaked out. She pressed every button, trying to make it stop, but it was no good. The elevator continued upward, and with each passing floor, the woman's stomach sank further. She knew exactly the destination. They were going to the tenth floor.

Upon reaching the tenth floor, the doors opened, but the woman did not step out. She had no desire to see this mysterious Otherworld. Even though it didn't look like a parallel dimension, just a regular office building, she took no chances. Instead, she hit the button for the first floor again, and nearly cried with relief when the elevator went down normally.

She nearly flew from the elevator on the first floor, coming out into the lobby. Instantly, she called her boyfriend, tearfully telling him what had happened. He laughed it off, believing her to be yanking his chain. She had been so dismissive and skeptical of the whole thing, he thought it impossible for her to suddenly turn about and become a believer. His words almost calmed her enough, at least, for her to sleep. He promised her that it would all be better in the morning.

The woman slept soundly that night, but in the morning, she woke as though in some kind of trance. Dazed, she crawled out of bed and found herself standing in an office. Unsure of what was going on, she began to wander around the office. There was nobody present. When she looked out the window, the sight shook her. The world was a wasteland, a hollow husk of building shells and grey streets. The only light came from far, far in the distance, but she didn't think it was the sun. Eager to get out, she spotted an elevator and headed for it. The sign above indicated that she was on the tenth floor. She pushed the button, and as the doors opened, an eerie sense of familiarity came over her. This was elevator she had played the game in. The elevator took her down to the lobby, and it was the exact same lobby as the day before. That was when she woke up.

This same dream has been plaguing the woman every night, from the first time she played to the time she posted the story. Sometimes the elevator is broken, and she has to take the stairs down. But the building is always the same, and the hollowed outside world is always there. She is not left alone during the day, either, for she sees the little blonde woman's face in crowds wherever she goes.

This is the woman's warning, for everyone. Even if you are a skeptic, don't play the Elevator Game. It is too risky and the supposed rewards don't matter in the grand scheme of things. Who wants to visit an Otherworld when one wrong step could mean you are trapped forever? For this is what the young woman believes has happened to her. She is trapped in the Otherworld.

Now, remember as you read the story, all the things she did wrong. First, she brought her cell phone with her. She acknowledged the fifth-floor woman, with eyes, hands, and words. Finally, and most importantly, she did not exit correctly. As with an Ouija board, if you do not end the game properly, the portal will stay open. In order to leave the Otherworld, you need to play all the steps of the Elevator Game again, visiting the floors in that same order.

She warns everyone not to play, but if you feel the curiosity burning, and you just have to try, at least learn from her mistakes.

CHAPTER EIGHT:
THE DEMON AT FORT SILL

A young marine named Logan and his buddy Richard was assigned to training at Fort Sill, Oklahoma. The compound, he describes, was quite large. But the specific area he and Richard were to be training at, the Battery was located next to a cemetery. Something that, looking back, Logan admits should have been the biggest red flag of them all.

For that was his entire first-day experience: red flags. But Logan was the kind of young man who didn't believe in ghosts, or the paranormal, or especially demons. So nothing that would have struck others as scary even registered on Logan's radar. For example, he didn't notice that the windows of the Battery were all barred. Instead, he and Richard headed right in. It was 1 in the morning, both young men were exhausted, and they were set to form ranks at 4:45 AM. They were assigned a first-floor room, 211, and headed down the hallway.

There, along the hallway, were two doors facing one another. They had a sign on them that read AUTHORIZED PERSONNEL ONLY. Laughing it off a bit, Logan and Richard joked about how they were going to sneak down there and see the restricted area. Most likely it was just weapons and artillery. As they walked past the door, however, the first strange thing happened. A loud bang went off, reminding Logan of a gunshot. Another marine stuck his head out of a doorway, snapping at them both to be quiet. Logan shook his head because it wasn't either of them. The sound, he stated, came from the basement.

At the very mention of said basement, all color drained from the marine's face. He looked up and down the hall, and quickly ushered Logan and Richard inside his room. Confused, the two young men followed him in. The marine shut the door, and sat down, forehead in his hands. He said the words that Logan would likely never forget: "You two have no idea what you're in for."

He went on to explain to the confused recruits that the three barrack buildings had all once served different functions. One was a psychiatric asylum, one was a morgue, and the building which they currently stood in had once held an electric chair in the basement. Logan didn't believe him at first, because none of this information was readily available to the public or to the recruited marines on the way, and they should have known that. But the marine pointed out the bars on the windows. No other barracks had bars.

The marine then went on to spin them a tale of his first night at Fort Sill. Two other marines had been playing around with an Ouija board in the basement and had gotten caught. Their superior officer confiscated the Ouija board away. Now, he believed that should be the end of it, but as the marine went on, he couldn't have been more wrong. The next morning, as it was his job to check on the superior officer and clean his office out, he went in. Apart from the officer, he was the only one in the building with a key. To his shock, he found the Ouija board sitting out flat on the desk.

The officer cut the board the shreds, but the next morning, it happened again. The Ouija board sat on the desk, unblemished. The superior officer, being a godly man, called in a priest to bless all three barracks. He then put the board in a chest of holy water and locked it in the basement. Since then, the marine finished, he has not been able to get a good night's sleep.

Logan was entertained by the story, but still didn't entirely believe it. He confirmed with the marine that the armory was also in the basement, just as he had suspected, which was the real reason why access was restricted. Satisfied, he and Richard continued on to their room. And for two weeks, everything seemed to pass completely normally.

Weekends gave the marines some free time, and as Logan and Richard hung out in their room, they made a terrible decision. They wanted to see if they could find that Ouija board. Armed with nothing but a screwdriver, they slipped out into the hall. It was around 11:00 PM, meaning just about everyone was asleep in their rooms. Quietly, they headed for the basement doors.

The boys were successful in prying open the doors with the screwdriver, and then they headed down into the basement. Only their phones served as a light source, and the air was cold—colder than it should have been. Logan could see his own breath before him, even though it was summer. He knew the air was wrong, and that there was no way it could be this cold, but yet again another red flag went ignored.

When they got into the room, Logan immediately noted that this was the room where the electric chair must have been. There was a metal plate on the ground, screwed in, and directly above it on the ceiling was a quick and dirty plaster job, just where wiring would have come down from the ceiling. He pointed this out to Richard, who instantly argued against that. They didn't know that for sure, he argued, "so be quiet." That was when a voice spoke from beside him.

The voice, Logan describes, was unlike anything he had ever heard before in his life. The words he used to describe it was "fingernails on a chalkboard, sandpaper across glass, almost excruciating to listen to." The only thing the voice said was, "leave."

Logan shouted and jumped, demanding to know what that was. Richard shushed him once again because they were going to get caught. But yes, he agreed quietly. He had heard the voice as well. Logan turned around, and saw a sight that filled him with such ice-cold dread and terror, he almost couldn't breathe.

Standing in the corner was a man—pitch black, so dark that the room seemed bright by comparison. He had one shadowed arm raised, and was pointing at the staircase. In that same voice, he commanded them again: "Leave, before you can't."

That was all it took for Logan and Richard to go running up the stairs, literally crashing through the basement door and out into the hall. Their on-duty supervisor came around the corner just as the door swung shut, and demanded to know what they were doing. Logan, too terrified to speak, wouldn't have even known how to answer in the first place.

Both boys had their liberties revoked, and spent the remainder of their days on the fort cleaning floors and scrubbing toilets. Upon graduating to the fleet, they left and never looked back. Logan warns that if he is ever asked to set foot in Fort Sill again, he will sooner go AWOL.

CHAPTER NINE:
TALES OF THE SKINWALKER

The Navajo Nation is a group of Native American people, living in the southwestern region of the United States, in states such as Arizona, Utah, and New Mexico. While Navajo history and folklore is wide and rich with stories passed down through tradition, one, in particular, has captured the minds of the paranormal community, and that is the legend of the skin-walker.

Known in the Navajo language as 'yee naaldlooshii,' the skin-walker is said to be a witch who wears the skins of animals then changes shape. When the Navajo use the term 'witch,' they do not mean it in the same European sense of a woman with a pointy hat who rides a broomstick. Usually men, but sometimes women, witches were exiles who used magic for harm. There are good witches in Navajo culture as well, who use their magic for healing. The same terms are not applied to them. A skin-walker represents everything that goes against Navajo cultural values, and there is a great reluctance among the Navajo community to speak of them in any sense—especially to non-Navajo outsiders.

Perhaps this mystery behind the legend is what led to its cultural transformation into something else by non-Navajo paranormal investigators. With no reliable information sources, the legend has spiraled and grown into something else entirely. Generally, on Internet forums, the difference lies in the dash between the words. Actual stories of Navajo skin-walkers will usually have the dash between the words 'skin' and 'walker.' For many trying to make sense of the horrifying things they see in the wilderness, they instead use the non-hyphenated title 'skinwalker.'

Most notably we can see the use of the word skinwalker as a nickname for the Utah reserve Sherman Ranch. It has become widely known as Skinwalker Ranch, a paranormal hot spot for strange sightings, ghostly encounters, and UFOs. But people have begun to share their stories of encounters with strange creatures in the desert. With no other name to give to these monsters, people have taken to calling them skinwalkers, as fitting or not as that name may be.

A girl living in a suburban area of the Midwest was about an hour's drive away from her boyfriend. On her way back home, she almost always takes the highway. After a day of hanging out with him, at around 11 PM, he decides he needs to go home since he has to get up for work the next day. She drives him home, taking the highway as usual. But on the way back, she makes a different decision than her usual. Turning left onto the back country roads, she decides to go for a little late-night drive around the countryside.

It was a cloudy, windy night. She couldn't see the stars, but they had the windows rolled down so the breeze would flow through the car. It was swerving a little in the wind. Though she considered turning on her high beams, she was cautious about blinding someone coming from the opposite direction.

Every single one of her choices thus far had been unlike her usual. Not only was she driving through an unusual route on a night with poor visibility, everyone driving through the backroads knows that you should turn on your high beams, and only turn them down if you see other headlights approaching in the distance. Whether it was just a pileup of these unusual decisions that led to her encounter, or something was somehow inclining her, she will never know.

Coming up to a hill, the area surrounding her car was split by a patch of woodland on the left, and rolling fields on the right. Up at the top of the hill, she saw an outline of a deer crossing the road. Coming closer, she saw the black antlered shape was bigger than a deer, and then thought maybe it was an elk. It was unusual, but not totally out of the ordinary for her area. But the closer she got, the more she could see the things that were wrong with it. The hulking creature was moving far too slowly and didn't even acknowledge the oncoming car.

She knew something was wrong. Again, she noticed that the creature was just too big, even for an elk. For an antlered creature, pretty much only a moose was that size, but there are no moose in the Midwest. She watched as it dragged itself toward the trees on her left, and the way it moved reminded her of a wounded animal.

Then, without warning, the thing whipped its head around to look at her. She almost screamed and hit the brakes. Close enough now to see its face, she was horrified.

The thing was in no way a deer or an elk. Its face was rotting, lips pulled back into a sneer and lined with sharp teeth. Some thick, dark substance drooled out from its mouth. Its eyes were like sunken, black holes, and they were staring right down at her.

She froze in terror, unable to move as she and creature were locked in a staring contest. She knew that she should move, throw the car into reverse and get out of there as fast as she possibly could, but that wasn't going to happen. She was completely stuck on the spot. Even when the hideous creature made a lurching move towards her car, she didn't move. She genuinely thought that this would be the end of her life, torn to shreds by some disgusting creature of the night. And even then, with that stark thought facing her down, she still could not make her hands move on the steering wheel, or lift her foot from the brake.

She was saved by another car coming up the hill from the opposite direction. They had their high beams on, and when those bright beams of light hit the creature, it let out a painful shrieking roar. With no further hesitation, it staggered the rest of the way into the woods on the left side of the road.

Free from the creature's spell, she slammed her foot on the gas and raced out of there. Dust flew up behind her and she was going well over the speed limit, but she didn't care. She knew that if she was still there after the other car had passed, that thing was going to come back out of the woods and right for her. So she booked it, as fast as she possibly could.

When she got home, in absolute hysterics, her family thought she had just seen a regular deer and was overreacting. The fear from almost hitting it was enough to make her exaggerate, they said. But she knew what she had seen. Her eyes would not play tricks on her like that. She did her study on skinwalkers, wondering if that was what it could have possibly been. If what she truly saw was a skinwalker, if it was a witch—like the original legends suggest—perhaps it manipulated the circumstances to turn up the way they did. But then, if that were the case, would it not also have manipulated the other car? Moreover, she lives in the Midwest, outside the general sighting area. While she does state that a skinwalker is her first guess, it begs the question: if that was not a skinwalker, then what was it?

Thankfully, when it came to research, she had a lot at her hands. There are new stories coming in every day of people who encounter skinwalkers. But not everyone has their encounters from the confines of a car. This one comes from a young man who works on a farm. One cool, crisp evening, he was out for a walk through the pastures when he found a trail of red. Now, for a city slicker, a trail of red would, of course, set you on high alert. But for those who live in the country, and especially anyone who lives on a farm, a trail of red just means an injured wild animal passed through. And that was exactly what this man believed it was, just an injured deer.

He continued on his walk and went on for several more hours. It was almost midnight when he decided to turn back. Behind him, his friend was standing in the road. He greeted him cordially, stating that he wanted to join him out for a walk.

Something didn't feel right about it all. That friend hardly ever joined the man on his walks, and it was already so late at night. Besides that, there was a putrid smell in the air, like that of rotting flesh and pus and blood. Moreover, it seemed to be emanating from his friend. The man wrinkled up his nose at it but asked him a few questions as though everything were normal. His friend answered the questions with ease, and although something still didn't seem quite right, he fell into step beside his friend as they walked back. Eventually parting ways, the man went back into his house and climbed into bed. In those moments before he fell asleep, an odd thought was poking at him. A funeral he had attended not too long ago. But before he could dissect that further, he fell fully asleep.

The next day, everything continued on as normal. The man went into town, bought some things here and there, filled his car up with gas, and returned home. As he was filling up his pantry, he turned on the TV. On the broadcast, they were talking about a man who had gone missing and whose body was found dead, but he didn't catch the name or the picture. Just as he was about to tune in to find out more, the signal cut off.

A little confused, but again shrugging it off, the man went out for his walk once again. As with the night before, he walked for hours, until once again his friend appeared just before midnight. With him came once again that horrible, putrid smell.

But this time, the man had been expecting it. For during the day, he had put the pieces together. That smell of death, the man on the television who had gone missing and been found dead, the funeral he attended but couldn't remember whose it was... It was his friend—this friend—the same one who is supposedly standing before him at midnight, on a back country road!

One of the more common and well-known legends surrounding skinwalkers is that they take on the shape of their most recent kill. They are also said to have a horrifying stench of death follow them. As he shone his flashlight on the creature, he saw its face clearly for the first time. It was not exactly his friend's face, but a rotting corpse of a copy. As the creature smiled, its legs began to extend. The man recalls that it had the look on its face of a killer who had just sighted their next victim.

He turned and ran, taking a path that led him off the road and into the trees. His flashlight bobbed and bounced, the light already beginning to grow dim and flicker. His batteries were running out. He stumbled and fell, checking over his shoulder to see if the thing was still chasing him. It was, but it had morphed from a ghostly copy of his dead friend into something much worse. All he saw was grey skin and bone in a creature that towered ten feet high. Adrenaline kicked him forward and he started to run again.

The skinwalker wasn't straining at all to catch him, which meant it was only trying to tire him out. The man was doing much the same. He knew he couldn't outrun the monstrosity, outright. But as the skinwalker seemed like it could run for hours without tiring, he knew he needed another option. As he turned around a sharp corner, the man climbed a tree. He hurriedly scuttled up it until he was above the creatures head.

When the skinwalker came around the corner, it stopped in place. It seemed confused. The man, hand pressed over his mouth to keep from making any noise, prayed that this plan of his would work. As the creature let out an annoyed screech and began looking around for him, the man quickly and quietly changed the battery on his flashlight. Taking the old battery, he chucked it as hard as he could. He heard the battery crashing in the trees up ahead, and the creature raced after it.

The man slid down from the tree and bolted in the opposite direction. He made it to the road, and through the dust that he kicked up, a herd of deer came bolting up behind him. He realized a second too late that the herd was also probably being chased by the creature, and he was right. The creature came up from behind him and caught one of the deer in its teeth.

Somehow, the dust cloud kicked up along the road proved enough of a cover for the man to make it back to his house. It was almost dawn by the time he got in the door. He threw the essentials in a truck and headed out of town so fast, he never once looked back.

He has told this story to everyone who will listen, but nobody believes him by the end of it. And in fairness, there are a lot of unbelievable things about his tale. But there seems to be a common thread among these stories of people not doing what they would normally do, or forgetting key points of information. If the legends are true and the skinwalkers really are using magic, it is not out of the realm of possibility that something is messing with people's minds. Leading them astray, and turning them into easier targets.

So if you ever find yourself walking alone in the southwestern portion of the United States, and find yourself doing something you wouldn't normally do, check yourself and turn back immediately.

CHAPTER TEN:

THE TALK ABOUT ZOZO

A group of friends once decided to play with an Ouija board, and strangely enough, the board began sending out words in Latin. Only one person in that group of friends could speak Latin, and he was not touching the planchette, so there was simply no way he could be making the words. Instead, he had to lean over and translate for the friends.

Eventually, the one who could speak Latin put his hand on the planchette, perhaps believing that the group was somehow playing a trick on him. Almost immediately, he pulled his hand away to reveal a bright red scratch on his wrist. No one knew where it came from, because no one had seen anything touch him. Nor, even, did anyone in the group of friends have red on their fingernails—as they would have to, given how deep the scratch went.

After a time, the entity they were contacting named itself 'Z.' One friend asked if Z was an enlightened being, to which the planchette responded in the affirmative. This friend, who was curious about this matter herself, asked how the being had opened all seven of its chakras.

At the top left corner of an Ouija board, there is a picture of a sun. At the bottom right, there is a picture of a medium. As the group of friends watched, the planchette began to move back and forth between the sun and the medium. It was almost moving at lightning speed. When the friend began to scream, "I get it! Talk to the sun!" the movement abruptly stopped.

The friends stopped playing, but for days after that, the girlfriend of the player who spoke Latin would wake up with bruises along her calves. She didn't know what they meant, or where they came from. After a few days, the one who had suggested the Ouija board in the first place quietly confessed something, something that made them swear to never pick up an Ouija board again: the entity Z seemed like it was trying to escape the board.

Many in the Ouija board community have tried to explain the truth about an entity known as Zozo. It is a demon that will try and come through an Ouija board and manipulates players into playing wrong so he can escape into our world. Many claims that Zozo is not real, just a fake story made up to go along with a fake game board. But there is more to the story of Zozo than you might think.

The main argument against the existence of Zozo is that he does not appear in any ancient or historical literature. Instead, the name is claimed to be derived from Pazuzu, the king of the demons in Mesopotamian mythology. Pazuzu's existence was popularized by the film 'The Exorcist,' which is where most trace back this concept of a demon named Zozo.

But not all mythologies need to be rooted in ancient history and dismissing Zozo because he only appears in modern urban legends is also dismissing other stories such as the Jersey Devil, and the technology-driven gremlins. Even the skinwalkers, which we've discussed in the last chapter, are more akin to modern desert monsters than they are to their Navajo originators. Monsters and demons can be born in our modern world just as they were born in the Dark Ages, or in 300 BCE. And considering that the Ouija board is a modern invention, it only makes sense that a modern demon would be born from the usage of it.

The earliest reference found serious problems caused by an Ouija board goes back to 1920. Taking place in a small town, in Southern California, the disturbance was noticed when the police were called to a house. Inside, they found seven people, completely in the nude and acting raving mad. In the house, the police found an Ouija board sitting on a table.

After that, the hysteria began rapidly spreading across town. Multiple people began stripping naked, including even a police officer, who ran unclothed into a bank and began screaming at anyone and anything. A fifteen-year-old girl, when questioned, told the authorities that her nude state was a side effect of being so attuned to the dead.

Terrified of the events and not knowing what to do about it, the few remaining authorities called in mental health specialists to come in and attend to all 1000 of the town's residents. Though it was attributed to mass hysteria, the authorities still took no chances and had all Ouija boards banned and burned.

To this day, no one knows what caused the residents to start taking their clothes off, as that is not something commonly attributed to using Ouija boards. It is, however, something that many relate to demonic encounters or possession. It could be that this little southern California town in 1920 was the birthplace of Zozo, the first time he was ever let out of the board.

One of the first stories where Zozo was stated by name came from a girl who had a direct encounter with the demon, who did refer to himself as Zozo.

She and her friend were having a sleepover one Saturday night and decided to have a play with the board. They quickly began receiving answers from the board, and the entity in the room with them identified itself as Zozo. The girl was not familiar with the name, but as soon as the board spelled it out, a chill went through her spine. The candle beside the board flickered out.

Instantly, her friend began to complain of a headache. Completely set on edge by these events, the girl ended the game quickly. Still, her friend complained of the pain in her head. It was like a migraine, but worse, she said. The two went to bed fairly quickly after that, hoping that things would all be better in the light of morning, and her friend would be able to sleep the headache off.

But in the middle of the night, things took a dark turn. The friend began sleepwalking and went right into the bedroom of her friend's little sister. Standing over her bed, she began shouting gibberish, a string of words that made absolutely no sense. The little sister woke immediately but was frozen in bed by the strange sight in front of her. This friend did not have a history of sleepwalking, also none of talking in her sleep. The gibberish she spoke wasn't like a normal, sleep talking gibberish, either. While usual talkers in their sleep string together words that make no sense but are words nonetheless. These girl's words were something else entirely like she was speaking in tongues. They got progressively louder and louder until she screamed "RED!" loud enough to wake the whole house.

The girl ran into her sister's room, but by the time she got there, her friend had disappeared. Together with her parents and little sister, they searched the house top to bottom. The friend was nowhere to be found. No one knew what they were going to tell the friend's parents. Had she run away? How had she escaped so quickly, when they all came running immediately after hearing her scream? The girl was far too afraid to admit to anyone that they had been playing around with an Ouija board.

After over half an hour of searching, the girl decided to take one last look in her own bedroom, which she had already searched thoroughly. But to her complete surprise, there was her friend—sleeping soundly as though nothing had happened. She didn't remember a thing about the night before.

All their parents wrote it off as simple sleepwalking, and the girl never admitted to playing with an Ouija board. She took her story to the Internet instead; warning against those who thought of playing with an Ouija board to contact Zozo might be a bit of fun. She doesn't know whether her friend was possessed, or whether Zozo was just playing around with them, but she knows she is afraid enough to never use an Ouija board again in her life.

But the most famous case of the Zozo demon came from a man named Darren Wayne Evans. In 2009, he posted on a true ghost encounters forum, first prefacing the reader with a warning that Ouija boards are not toys, and should not be played with lightly under any circumstances. Many believe that Evans was the creator of the Zozo demon legend, but he insists that this could not be further from the case, and to this day is trying to prove to the community that Zozo has existed for longer than 2009.

Evans goes on to tell that he used Ouija boards quite regularly, and one entity that he made constant contact with named itself Zozo. The following account seems to ring true for almost every encounter with Zozo. At first, he came across as very nice, answering any questions presented to him and even performing tricks such as moving small objects, telling the exact time, or snuffing out a candle. But, as with every story, he gradually turned quite nasty. Cussing, cursing, and spitting all sorts of black insults to the users playing with the board. It threatened others in the room, even those who weren't playing with the board, and cursed several times in Latin and Hebrew. At least, those were the languages to Evans' knowledge, for he spoke neither of them and was too afraid to repeat the curses and insults, aloud or on paper, lest they be dangerous.

But still, Evans continued to contact Zozo. He was fascinated by the way the spirit would swap moods, going from kind and friendly one minute, to cursing him out the next. Zozo even used a number of biblical insults against him.

Seemingly, this goes in direct contrast to what most say about demons. They cannot speak words of the bible, just as they fear the cross and burn upon contact with holy water. Remember, though, that demons are not restrained to Christian mythology and instead pop up in folklore from all around the world. The original Pazuzu was of Mesopotamian origin. Besides that, it would certainly make sense for a modern demon to have all the common attributes of a classic demon, but none of the weaknesses.

After a time, the threats grew even darker. And Zozo seemed to lock in on a target—Evans' girlfriend. He continually spoke of how he wanted to possess her and take her to paradise. When Evans asked Zozo what he believed paradise was, the board spelled out HELL. When Evans noticed his girlfriend would sometimes fall into a trance-like state, he feared that Zozo had gotten his way and was now possessing her.

After that, the activity spiraled out and away from the board itself. Evans caught his daughter, who was only one year old, drowning in the tub. He pulled her out just in time. His girlfriend claimed that she had been running the girl a bath, and just wandered out of the room for a second. The water had then risen up above the baby's level. The very next day after that, the same daughter was hospitalized with an unexplainable infection. She was put into isolation for 14 days, and Evans recalls that they almost lost her.

His girlfriend's behavior began to mimic that of Zozo, going from sweet and caring one minute, to cruel and detached the next. The strangeness around the house continued as well, with guests hearing voices coming through the walls. His girlfriend's brother, who lived with them at the time, complained that he could not sleep at night due to the loud conversations. Evans made the activity stop for a while, by shouting a blessing in the name of God one night. He claims a shuddering vibration went through his house, rattling even the windows.

After that, he and his girlfriend broke up, and Evans moved to Michigan to begin a relationship with someone he met online. This new girlfriend didn't believe in ghosts or demons. Evans made the mistake of trying to convince her, purchased another Ouija board, and once again made contact with Zozo. The events played out just the same as they had before.

Evans has his own website, and his experiences were sold to the rights of aspiring filmmakers, leading many to accuse him of making it all up for the attention. But Evans remains adamant that it is all real, and continuously cautions anyone from making contact with Zozo. As for himself, he says that he won't even speak the entity' name aloud anymore, for fear of letting it draw power.

As for whether you believe that Zozo is a real entity, that is up to you. Most are skeptics, and still even many in the paranormal community who believe in the power of Ouija boards completely dismiss Zozo as a fantasy. But do your research, read the stories, and make the decision for yourself. Do you wonder if enough collective belief in a certain thing can bring it into existence? Do humans have that kind of psychic power? Take the moment to really think about it. And whether you actually believe in Zozo or not, please at least take the words of Darren Wayne Evans to heart: the Ouija board is not a toy.

CHAPTER ELEVEN:
ONE MISSED CALL

Headlines were made when a 2014 movie, 'Unfriended,' made a success for itself by being filmed entirely through Skype. The movie, which tells the story of a group of friends contacted by the ghost of their recently deceased friend, was panned by some and praised by others. But the idea that the deceased can contact you through technology is not an original concept at all. For decades, people have been reporting cases of calls from the dead.

There are two kinds of calls from the dead a person can receive. In one case, a person will receive a call from a friend or relative. Usually, they find out later that this person had passed away before the call was placed, but sometimes the call will come after the person has been long deceased. In almost all cases, however, the phone calls instead come from a number listed as 000-000-0000. In these cases, reports come in of hearing static on the other line. Usually, these calls come in the days preceding or following a funeral.

And these stories are not just recent phenomena, either. The earliest story dates back to a man named David Wilson in 1913, who began receiving strange messages on his wireless telegraph. It was designed to use the Morse code system, a series of dot and dashes to make coded messages. The messages began coming through, he claimed, even after the wire had been cut. Gathering witnesses, Wilson began to jot down what the codes were saying, and translating them. The messages he got chilled him to the bone. "Great difficulty, await message, five days, six evening." "Wait until next Tuesday." The messages were instructional in nature, but nothing ever came from them. Moreover, they frightened him, because he had no idea where they were coming from. Wilson invited scientists and experts to study his machine, and try to find out where these strange messages were coming from. No one could figure it out, and a source was never traced back. After that, David Wilson seems to disappear from all record.

Even Thomas Edison himself thought that, if spirits existed, the telephone would prove the most effective way to communicate. Though he was reluctant about it and made no bold claims, he certainly supposed that the delicacies of telephone airwaves would be more open for communication with a spirit world or parallel dimension. There are even rumors that Edison tried to build a spirit telephone.

There is a particularly chilling story by a poster named Mary, who recalls her experience as a telephone sales representative. She discloses that she was marketing a phone service, and was making calls to Pennsylvania. On this particular day, she called the home of a Mr. & Mrs. B. She does not disclose their full surname. The one who picked up the phone was Mrs. B, an older woman who seemed very interested in the product. Though she asked many questions, Mary recalls that whenever she tried to push the sale, Mrs. B would back out. She needed to speak to her husband about it first. Mrs. B goes on to explain that Mr. B was retired, and had been married to one carrier all his life and refused to make any changes. Again and again, Mary tried to encourage her to make a purchase, as she was trained to do, but again Mrs. B would always deflect to her husband.

Nothing about the call was out of the ordinary; it was the kind of conversation Mary had with little old ladies all the time. After all, they were the ones most likely to keep talking, and not immediately hang up the phone. The two eventually came to an agreement, since Mrs. B was so interested in the product but did not want to make the decision without her husband's consent. He would always leave early in the morning for fishing, as it had been his favorite activity since retirement, and the sales rep should call again early before he left. Satisfied that it would be worth the callback since Mr. & Mrs. B would most likely make the purchase, Mary left it at that.

When she called back the next morning, however, she was hit with a shock like a bucketful of cold water. Mr. B answered the phone, and when Mary began discussing the conversation of the day before, Mr. B had no recollection. He then went out to gruffly shout that his wife had died recently, and he had no idea what she was going on about. He slammed his receiver down, leaving Mary in shock, wondering who she had spoken to the day before, and why they had held a conversation for so long. Mary had never believed in ghosts before that, but now she most certainly does.

But as technology advances forward, so do the methods by which a spirit can choose to communicate with us. For example, it has been noted that Facebook is a common way for the dead to try and communicate with their friends and family. Most often, a person's Facebook account will not be closed immediately after they die, and sometimes messages from that account will begin sending out. Though this is often claimed to be the work of hackers, this begs the question of why a hacker would do something like that. Nothing can be gained by accessing the account of a deceased person and sending out messages, other than one's own sick pleasure, I suppose.

Other stories include messages sent to a deceased persons account and being marked 'seen,' indicating that someone has been on the account and seen these messages. While some see that as Facebook making a mistake, perhaps not memorializing the account properly, others see it as a confirmation that their deceased loved ones are still with them in spirit, watching and listening.

But more common in recent years than phone calls or even Facebook messages have been ghostly text messages. And while most stories of phantom telephone calls involve innocent, even heartwarming exchanges between the living and the deceased, the stories from haunted text messages are not usually so sweet. In fact, a very recent story involves a girl named Lindsay, living in Washington, and receiving a host of rather disturbing text messages.

She was at home by herself one evening in the summer, watching TV and playing around on her phone, when a text notification popped up. The message read: "Linzy i c u." It was from a number she didn't have in her contacts, nor was it any from a known friend or family member. Lindsay instinctively looked around, but she was on the second floor, and her blinds were drawn. She even checked through them to see if anyone stood on the street outside, but there was no one. She was completely alone.

Sitting back on the bed, Lindsay responded to the text, asking who it was. In return, she got yet another eerie reply. *"Just a friend. sum1 who watches ur every move. ur lil guardian angle."*

At this point, Lindsay knew this could not be any one of her friends. Nobody she knew texted like this, with such a particular pattern, and nobody would misspell a word as simple as "angel." They had also misspelled her own name. She responded to the number as such, again asking who they were. She knew they were no friend of hers, repeating the aforementioned evidence. To this, the number only replied that it didn't matter who it was, and asked if Lindsay was having fun watching TV.

Chills went down Lindsay's spine after reading this. How would anyone know she was watching TV? They could not see inside her room unless whoever was texting

her was also inside the house. Hurriedly, she ran around checking every door and window. Everything was locked, just as she suspected, and there was no one else in the house. Lindsay threatened to call the police if the texter did not tell her their identity, to which she got the most frightening response of all: "Good luck with that. I am standing right next 2 u but nobody will ever find me."

Again, Lindsay looked around on instinct. And again, there was nobody there. The room was empty. Now getting afraid for her life, Lindsay took the house phone and called the unknown number. As she feared, she was met with the dreaded 'not in service' voice mail. She stared down at her cell phone, wondering if the texts would stop, hoping that the texter had simply run out of minutes and that was why their number was out of service. To her dismay, another text came in complimenting her newly dyed blonde hair.

At this point, Lindsay really did call 911. She had only dyed her hair a few days ago, and she had not even updated all her pictures on social media. The only possible way the texter could have known was if they really were able to see her. As she tearfully explained her situation to the operator, she continued to stare down at her phone. The operator assured her that someone would come by to check on the house. Lindsay thanked them, hung up, and instantly received another message.

"Linzy, why did you have to do that?"

Apart from still spelling her name incorrectly, the spelling pattern of the texter had changed. Lindsay didn't know if this meant the texter had gotten angry—she hoped not but suspected that was indeed the case. She asked what she did, and got the reply that she knew what she did. Nobody was going to help her or believe her; the messages went on, attacking Lindsay personally. She continued to repeat her question, asking again who this was. Eventually, she got her final answer. "U will c. someday."

A knock came at the door, and Lindsay screamed, but it was only the police officer there to check over her house. He confirmed what she already knew in her heart: that the house was empty. No one was inside, and no one had been inside recently, except for Lindsay.

She showed the messages to the police officer and was advised to simply turn off her phone while they looked into it. Lindsay did, and the messages stopped. At the time of posting her story, she had received no new messages but had also received no news from the police about the number, either. Unfortunately, in most cases like this, the mysterious phone number will go ignored. It is unlikely Lindsay will ever know who, or what was texting her.

All this evidence goes hand in hand with the modern ghost hunter's use of a spirit box and an EMF reader. Knowing that ghosts have an easier time accessing these frequencies lends credence to them, and certainly to the messages they portray. Electronic voice phenomena, the experiences of people who heard voices of the dead through any electronic device such as television, radio, and yes—phones, have a new wave of believability behind them when you consider that stories of the dead making phone calls trace all the way back to 1913. For as long as people have been developing technology, ghosts have been attempting to communicate to us through them. And as the future progresses and we see more and more advanced technology at our fingertips, these communications may continue to become easier. Perhaps one day, Edison's rumored spirit telephone will even become a reality.

CHAPTER TWELVE:
IT FOLLOWED

This story comes to me directly from an anonymous source, from a woman who has never before shared her story in public—not on any online forums, and hardly even to family and friends. When questioned why, the woman, under the pseudonym Jane, stated: "I think because I always believed everyone would accuse me of making it up. There's a level of distrust when it comes to sharing experiences with the paranormal, even the ones you trust the most. Either people are going to believe you've made it all up for attention, or that you misinterpreted the events in some way. To which I would like to reply that it's pretty difficult to misinterpret events like this."

After years of sitting on her story and wanting to tell it truthfully, but not knowing the proper place for it to make the most impact, Jane has brought it to my doorstep. By having it here, in this book, Jane knows people will believe her.

Jane's elementary school was infamous among its students for having a haunted girls' change room. Teachers never talked about it, and it certainly wasn't advertised, but by the time you reached the age of eight, the rumor would have reached your ears. Of course, it was particularly more prevalent among girls, who had to spend time in the change room before and after every gym class. It was impossible to be in a room known for its hauntings, and not talk about it.

Change rooms are places where time seems to stand still, haunted or not. They are a place where people are at their most vulnerable. With no adult supervision and this closed-off atmosphere of twilight, it became the ripest of moments for ten-year-olds to be messing with the paranormal.

A group of girls, not Jane's friends, decided to play a game of Bloody Mary. There was a bathroom connected to the rest of the change room, with big mirrors that were perfect for the game. At this age, Jane had only ever vaguely heard of the game, and she didn't know anything about the rules or consequences. The warning siren that goes off in your head, telling you that perhaps playing a game with demons in a place known for spiritual activity is not a good idea—that alarm doesn't exist at the age of ten. So Jane, curious as to what all the fuss was about, joined the crowd around the door to the bathroom.

The girls turned out the lights in the bathroom, leaving awash in the half-light coming through the open door. They spoke three times: "Bloody Mary, Bloody Mary, Bloody Mary." They turned around three times in a circle. And... nothing happened. No demonic witch came screaming out of the mirror to take their eyes. Later, Jane would learn that they had played the game wrong, and perhaps the only thing that stopped them all from being cursed was their own ignorance. At the time, she was more interested in the history of the real Bloody Mary, sister of her favorite queen, Elizabeth I. Jane went on to read about the Tudor era and largely forgot about the whole incident.

Until a few months later, when it all came back to her. She and a friend were the last two left in the change room one day after gym, lingering behind so they could talk and gossip in the empty, echoey room. The talk turned, as it always seemed to, towards the ghosts in the change room. Jane's friend turned and pointed to the always-locked door at the far end of the room. That, she claimed, is where the ghosts lived.

Jane knew, vaguely, that behind the locked door were the showers. She had never been the inquisitive type and never questioned why a change room would have showers that were always locked. But as her friend began to spill rumors—rumors of ghostly incidents and injuries that lead to the showers being locked off—Jane found herself questioning it as well. In the midst of all the stories being thrown at her, Jane asked a single question: Why don't we try and open it?

In bare feet, the two girls approached the door. Jane's heart was pounding, but it wasn't fear. She was excited. In her mind, Jane believed that nothing would really happen. Nothing had happened all those months ago when they played Bloody Mary, so why should anything be different now? She was just going to pull on the doorknob and nothing would happen, they could both laugh at themselves, and go back to class with a story.

Jane's hand closed over the doorknob. She doesn't remember whether the metal was cool or warm, focused only on the act of turning it—because, to Jane's great surprise, it didn't stop her. The door, suddenly, wasn't locked. The knob turned. Jane began to pull it, and the door opened a single centimeter. Through the crack, she could just make out shapes in the darkness beyond. That was when, without warning, the door pulled back out of her grasp. Pulled, Jane remembers. She didn't let go. The knob twisted in her grip, then yanked backward, as though someone on the other side had pulled it out of her grasp. The door slammed shut, with a loud bang that echoed in tandem with the girls' screams. That was when Jane saw it. To the right of the door was the light switch. As all the lights in the change room flickered on and off, one of the switches physically moved down, and back up.

Jane grabbed her shoes and ran, friend hot on her heels. Bare feet slapping on the linoleum floors, shoes in hand, Jane tried to make sense of what she had seen. She and her friend were giggling through their fear, half whispering and half shrieking. Along the hall, one teacher leaned out of a classroom to tell them to be quiet and get to class. "Did you see the lights?" asked her friend.

She had certainly seen them flicker. Had the switch actually gone up and down like that? Or was that her mind, playing tricks on her? She wanted to believe that she was over exaggerating, that the flickering lights had caused her to see something that wasn't really there. But her heart knew that switch had moved on its own.

Jane wouldn't know it at the time. But looking back, that day was the last time she ever felt alone.

Jane and her friend never spoke of the incident to anyone, and gradually they drifted apart, as friends in elementary school often do. They haven't spoken in over ten years now, and Jane doubts the other would remember the incident so vividly. But Jane never forgot her experience. She thought about it every day, the memory remaining crystal clear.

Yet as she kept her story quiet, over the years, the same would not prove so for the friends she made in high school. They loved sharing their stories. One, in particular, suffered from sleep paralysis and was subjected to visions of shadow men. That was how it came up: sometimes, they felt as if someone was watching them. They were not alone. Jane understood what the meant—she always felt watched. Especially at night, when Jane was positive there was something in her bedroom, in the dark. It didn't even scare her half the time, because she was just so used to it. But gradually Jane felt the difference between her experiences and those of the people around her. The feeling of not being alone never went away. By this time, looking back, Jane realized that she didn't even remember what it felt like to be alone.

And so it continued on in that way for years. Whether she'd be doing homework in her room, out for a neighborhood walk, and especially in public bathrooms, Jane felt the presence of something looking over her shoulder. She became accustomed to the action of looking behind her. She sang to herself to lower the oppressive silence. Mostly, she tried not to think about what was watching her. She didn't know whether it was a ghost that had latched onto her, a poltergeist, or a demon. She hadn't made the connection between the elementary school change room and held a belief that the thing was a part of her house. But she was still smart enough to refuse any games of Bloody Mary or an Ouija board.

The worst of it came at night. More often than not, Jane was unable to sleep. Despite not ever seeing anything, fear would creep into her thoughts. Her heart would begin to pound, sometimes so violently, that it would leave her dizzy and light-headed. Several times, she had to get up at 2 in the morning and turn on a light. After this happened too many times, Jane kept a flashlight beside her bed so she could shine a light on the shadows. She didn't know how to make it stop, because she was still determined not to tell anyone. The rational part of her brain believed that it could all be explained away through science. Fear of the dark was making her see things that weren't there.

Jane was also an avid camper. When she began hearing footsteps and seeing shadows outside her tent, Jane knew the entity was not connected to her house. It was connected to her—following her. And finally, Jane made the connection between her current haunting and the day in the change room. This being, whatever it was, had been let out that day when she opened the door and it had latched onto her. Terrified but now resolute, Jane tried her best to dig into research. She found no information about kids dying on her elementary school property, so she quickly ruled out the idea that it was a simple ghost haunting her. Unfortunately, that would have been the best option. Jane spent a brief period of time believing she was the target of a poltergeist, but as she studied more history of the poltergeist, she threw that theory out as well. Apart from the one light switch, nothing had ever moved on its own in Jane's presence. Moreover, she had a fairly happy home life and did not suffer from any of the usual symptoms children displayed, such as behavioral problems, the poltergeists usually latched on to. This left Jane with her final, and worst, conclusion: that she was being stalked by some kind of demon.

Still, Jane sometimes believed she was crazy. Whenever she was in broad daylight, surrounded by friends, the whole thing seemed laughable. Jane knew how stories of demon hauntings worked. She had seen movies. She knew that her experiences should be more intense than just bad feelings that kept her from sleeping.

Around the time she figured it was a demon, Jane also began to notice strange noises. At first, she thought they would come from around her, but more often than not they seemed to originate from inside her own ears. She would hear a low, dull humming, like some kind of low register machine. Jane had always had a very sensitive hearing, but she often attributed the buzzing in her ears to an after effect of listening to music so loud. But after her demonic revelation, Jane began listening for the differences in the buzzing. When she took out her headphones after listening to her music, it was always more of a high pitched whine. The low humming was a completely different tone, and she felt it in a different part of her ears. Moreover, she never heard it after taking out her earbuds. So it became clear to her that they were two separate things. After that, Jane started thinking about what other things she had always attributed to something else—like her ears popping. Jane's ears popped so often, her frequent attempts to unblock them by sniffing and blowing her nose got on people's nerves.

Jane, too, had a long history of her feet cramping. By the time she was twelve, Jane couldn't even point her toes without them cramping horribly. This affected her performance in gym class and could make swimming difficult at times. While Jane had never before considered this to be an effect of her ghostly encounter, and to this day, she doesn't know if it is or not, she knew muscle cramps were a part of demonic possession.

Jane was not an overly religious person, and she still didn't really attribute demons to God. Jane was a reader and a big fan of world mythologies, so she knew demons could come from any corner of mythology. So she didn't rely on any religious talismans to protect her. Instead, Jane had a talisman. Such a funny little thing, but it always seemed to work: her teddy bear. Jane had slept with a teddy bear since she was a baby, and she took it everywhere with her. It was one of the only things she was never ashamed of, not even when she went to high school and people started questioning her. What kind of sixteen-year-old still sleeps with her teddy bear? To which Jane has always replied coolly that she doesn't get nightmares, so who is the true winner in the situation?

And it was true. For all the strange things that happened to Jane, she never had nightmares. And when she felt a presence with her, she didn't always feel like it was a threatening presence. Jane still thinks that the reason her encounter with the demon never reached drastic levels was that her teddy bear was somehow holding it at bay.

Everything changed on the day the hauntings came to a head. Jane was walking home from school one day in her senior year. That particular semester, her last period was a free period, and so she always went home alone instead of walking with a friend. And, because it was so early, the mass of students leaving the high school wasn't present. Instead, Jane would be let out with maybe twenty students, most of whom took the bus instead of walking.

On this particular day, Jane checked behind her, as she had become so accustomed to every day. And she noticed a boy walking behind her. He wasn't close; he was a bit far down the path. Certainly not close enough to make out any facial features. Jane could see that he wore a baggy black hoodie and black pants. Something about him set Jane on edge, but she couldn't figure it out and kept walking forward. Perhaps it was the black pants because almost everyone in Jane's town wore jeans. Perhaps it was his hood, which was pulled up, something Jane wasn't used to seeing. Whatever it was, the familiar feeling crept back into Jane's limbs, causing her heart rate to increase and her head to feel a little faint. After another thirty seconds of walking, Jane looked behind her again.

The boy behind her had kind of a gangly walk, but he wasn't looking at his feet, like most people. His face was turned upwards, death-pale. Jane's stomach curdled as she tried to make out his features, but her eyes skated right over them.

He didn't have a face.

Not in the sense that his head was a blank slate. It was worse than that, somehow. His face was lumpy, and there were supposed to be facial features there, but Jane just wasn't seeing them. There was something there, there had to be because he was looking right at her. But as for his eyes, nostrils, mouth? It all just looked like putty.

Jane was too afraid to start running. She didn't want this thing to know she was afraid. But she did try to walk faster and continued to look behind her. The thing was still following her, still walking its strange gangly walk, still the same distance away.

Her house was up a hill and through the forest, and once she hit the treeline, Jane stopped looking back. As soon as she passed through the forest and hit her street, Jane finally broke out into a run. She ran until she reached her door, wrenched it open, and slammed it shut behind her. She locked it, and, too afraid to do anything—lay on the couch and tied not to faint.

Jane listened for anything at the door, but nothing happened. And since that day, nothing has happened since. Jane doesn't know exactly how, or why, but it was as if she managed to outrun the demon. She never saw any boys who looked gangly and clad in all-black, hanging around her school, so there was no one she could have confused for a demon.

It has been six years since then, and Jane has gradually stopped looking over her shoulder as much. But she still gets that strange, creeping fear every once in a while at night. She still hears deep thrums and her ears pop most days of the week. She still sleeps with a cell phone under her pillow, so she can shine a light around her dark room whenever she needs to. She still sleeps with her teddy bear.

And she still never feels alone.

CHAPTER THIRTEEN:
THE VALLECAS HAUNTING

Despite being one of the most well documented true stories of a demonic possession in recent years, the story of the Vallecas Haunting has little traction and hardly anyone knows about it. There was even a movie adapted from the true story, and while that always makes stories blow up, the 2017 Spanish movie 'Veronica' was a moderate commercial success, and the case did not gain any more traction. So the scariest story has been saved for last. Here, you will find the full story recounting the events of the Vallecas Haunting.

Vallecas is a small town near Madrid, in Spain. In the year 1990, the father of Concepcion Gutierrez was in the hospital, on the verge of death. Concepcion had gathered her children to the hospital, hoping they could have one last visit with their grandfather. To outward appearances, this was a cherished family gathering, a time to send thoughts and prayers to a man on his deathbed. But to those on the inside, it was only a cold, obligatory visit. Concepcion's father was known for being cruel, and there was no one he hated more than his own grandchildren. Nobody knew why, for if there was any reason for his intense hatred, it was a secret that went to the grave with him.

There at the hospital that day, was Concepcion's eldest teenage daughter; Estefania Gutierrez Lazaro was eighteen, pretty, social, and full of life. Thinking of this bright young girl, who by all accounts was beloved by her parents, siblings, and schoolmates, it is hard to imagine that any grandfather would not be proud to call her family. Yet, Concepcion's father showed no remorse or change of heart.

In case you have any questions or believe her grandfather's hatred has something to do with some scandal involving Estefania's last name, I will take a brief interlude to explain how Spanish surnames work. In most Spanish-speaking countries, a person has two last names: their father's family name, and their mother's maiden name. This is why, in many English reports, you will see the family referred to as either the Gutierrez family or the Lazaro family. Both of these are simultaneously correct, and incorrect.

Now, to the deathbed of Concepcion's father—even on the verge of facing God in heaven, he was unwilling to repent his hatred. There are even reports that he had Estefania lean down to him, so he could whisper in her ear: "If I cannot harm you in this life, I will do it in the next one." This is unconfirmed, but given the events that followed, it seems more than likely to be a true threat he made.

In the months that followed, Estefania's life continued on as normal. She didn't think so much about her grandfather or his threats, instead focusing on school and her friends. But only a few months after the death of her grandfather, a tragedy struck Estefania's group of friends. One of them had a boyfriend, who died in a motorcycle accident. He had been taken so suddenly, Estefania's friend was devastated that she would never talk to him again. She had not even been given the chance to say goodbye. That was around the time the group of friends discovered a way to contact him. You may have already guessed it. They decided to attempt to use an Ouija board.

One day, during school hours, the group of friends gathered around and attempted to start a séance. They did not get very far before being caught by a teacher. The Ouija board was instantly confiscated, but the group of friends had not gotten a chance to properly say goodbye. To the surprise and horror of everyone watching, the teacher broke the Ouija board in half. The friends had been using a glass as a planchette, and teacher smashed that as well. From the broken glass, a thick black smoke emerged. The smoke was then directly inhaled, albeit accidentally, by Estefania.

In the weeks following, Estefania's parents noticed a rapid change in her behavior. They reported her conditions to several doctors in the area, telling them all the same thing. Estefania would burst into unprovoked rages, turning on her younger brothers. She suffered from seizures. She would foam at the mouth, and her eyes were noted to sometimes roll all the way back into her skull. She began to have hallucinations, moaning to her mother that she could see shadows in her room, walking around through the night.

None of the doctors were able to diagnose her condition properly. Though it was suspected that epilepsy was the root of her seizures and hallucinations, all tests proved inconclusive and Estefania seemed biologically very healthy. Besides, even if Estefania had been diagnosed epileptic, there was no explanation as to why she would suddenly develop this disorder. With nothing medical to be done and Estefania's condition worsening every day, there was nothing Concepcion and her family could do but watch. In August of 1991, Estefania Gutierrez Lazaro passed away. Medically, it was ruled as a heart attack. She was just nineteen.

Her condition was ruled as a sudden onset of psychosis. It was after Estefania's death that her grieving parents heard the story of the Ouija board from her friends. A new theory began to circulate about Estefania's strange behavior, this time believing that she had been possessed and that somehow, the spirit of her late grandfather was at fault.

The trials of Concepcion Gutierrez were not over. In fact, they had only just begun. In the days following Estefania's death, Concepcion began to hear odd knocking sounds around her house. Often, these knocks would originate from Estefania's old room. Once, when the noises got particularly harsh, she checked in on them only to find Estefania's possessions thrown about the room. People in the family, including her younger sons, began to see the same shadowy figures that had plagued Estefania before her death. Concepcion could hear voices in her hallways—a girl's voice crying, *"Mama, Mama"* and the chilling laughter of an old man.

The house was continually plagued by temperature fluctuations and other odd phenomena. Conception's husband, Maximo, recalled one of the worst events that he witnessed himself. He was playing with one of his sons, Maximilian, when the boy was suddenly lifted into the air. Before Maximo could say or do anything, he was thrown violently across the room. Luckily, Maximilian was unharmed, but the event had shaken both he and his father.

Another chilling event happened when the family was gathered in the living room, watching TV. The door burst open, and horrible knocking sounds came again, all up and down the walls. The family shut the door and barricaded it with the sofa, even placing a heavy marble ornament on top of it for extra fortifications. This would all prove in vain. A strange gust of wind surged through the door, blowing the marble ornament, the sofa, and all the members of the family across the living room. Conception recalls that, in the wind, a single item was blown into the room with them: a framed photograph of Estefania. As Concepcion picked up the photograph, she was horrified when it began to burn in her hands. The fire spread through the photograph, burning down the center of Estefania's face. The frame remained cold, and Concepcion's hands were unharmed. The burned photograph was kept as evidence.

They were not the only ones to witness the paranormal events. People who came to visit the house would often experience the same phenomena. Concepcion's sister recalls sleeping there one night, and the in the darkness, she saw a blackened figure crawling across the floor, dragging itself by its arms, towards her.

The house became well-known throughout the community for its hauntings and was visited by mediums, priests; anyone the family believed could help them. There are several reports by local priests, claiming the house was indeed haunted by a malevolent spirit. During the visit of one psychic medium, the woman supposedly became possessed by the spirit of the grandfather. The event was part of a news broadcast and was televised. During the broadcast, viewers could see the medium attack those around her, a crazed look in her eyes. After returning to herself, she informed Concepcion and family that the spirit of the grandfather was indeed haunting them, but Estefania's spirit was fighting back against him. She had stayed behind from moving on to the next life to protect them.

But despite all the investigations, no one could offer any help to the family. Things continued to escalate until November of 1992 when Maximo Gutierrez finally had enough. He called the police, telling them straight out that his house was haunted, and his family's life was in danger. What prompted this call had been Concepcion, woken in the middle of the night to feel a pressure on top of her, and hands grabbing at her ankles and pulling.

The police were baffled about what to do. People didn't usually call in for a haunted house. Maximo continued to beg with them, finally passing the phone around each member of his family, asking them to describe what they were seeing. Through the static of the phone came the frantic reports that all the crosses in the house were turning upside down.

Hearing the panicked state the family was in; officers were dispatched and sent to the Gutierrez household. One was Inspector Jose Negri, who took charge of the case. He took three other officers with him. When he arrived on the scene, Negri saw the parents and two young boys standing out in the cold, too frightened to go back inside. Negri gave their home a brief inspection but saw outwardly nothing that would cause such distress. There were no signs of a break-in, no great messes.

As he sat down with the married couple in the living room, Negri listened to Concepcion recount all the things that had happened in the last year. Negri ordered two officers to stay in the living room with her, while he went out and searched the rest of the house more thoroughly. It was inside the parents' bedroom that Negri and his officers heard the first of the noises: a loud crash that sounded as though something had fallen onto the balcony. This was followed by a rolling sound, going across the balcony's floor. But when Negri checked outside, he saw nothing.

He went back into the living room, to ask if the other officers had also heard the noise. None of them had. As they stood around, unsure of what to do, they witnessed the next account. A pine armoire was sitting in the corner, and one of its doors flew open. An officer was standing next to it and would have been clocked on the head if his partner hadn't shouted for him to get out of the way.

It was at this point Negri and his officers began to get nervous. They had all pulled their guns, but they were pointed at furniture. Negri gave the armoire a brief inspection but could find no strings, wires, or other mechanisms that would have caused the armoire to open.

Two of the officers took after the family and left the house. They chose instead to stand outside in the cold. The police cars had drawn the attention of several neighbors, who gathered outside to see what was going on. As the officers interviewed them, the neighbors all corroborated the story. They remembered Estefania's deterioration and death the year prior, and many had seen strange shadows along the walls of the house. Through the windows, they reported seeing objects fly around.

Inside the house, Negri inspected Estefania's old room. He could see a crucifix lying on the floor, and the spot on the wall where it had been violently ripped from the nail. One of the posters that hung on Estefania's wall had been torn to shreds, hanging from the empty crucifix nail. Negri also took note of the strange, crimson goo that had begun to form around the furniture in the house. When he pointed this out, Concepcion tearfully admitted that she had never seen that goo before.

Finally, Negri went into the room which the family described to him as the worst: the bathroom. It seemed that the paranormal encounters in this particular room had gotten so bad, the family was no longer using it as a bathroom, and instead only to store extra dishes when needed. Instantly upon entering, he felt the temperature drop in the room. The hair on his neck stood on end.

That was all it took for Negri to leave the house as well. He gathered the family outside and admitted that there was nothing the police could do about the phenomena. With no choice left to them, Concepcion and Maximo took their two sons and left Vallecas. They have reported that the paranormal activity did not follow them, and no other strange events have happened at the house since. It seemed that whatever was tying the spirits of Estefania and her grandfather to that house, lifted when the family moved away. Concepcion and her family can only pray that Estefania's spirit is finally at peace.

When Negri filed his official report for the proceedings, he left nothing out and explained in detail all the strange phenomena witnessed at the Gutierrez household. This was surprising to everyone at the time, since police are notorious for never including the paranormal in their reports. Even more surprising, all the witnessing officers signed the report as well. Negri was unable to come up with any sort of logical explanation for the things he saw, and the stories he heard. This makes the Vallecas Haunting one of the most legitimate hauntings in history. It was corroborated not only by friends and family, but neighbors, the priesthood, psychics, and even the police. No other case in modern history has so many viewpoints that all agree with one another, making the Vallecas Haunting a case like no other.

CONCLUSION

What's incredible about the entire idea of demons and demonic possession is just how prevalent the phenomenon is throughout the world. Beliefs and experiences of encounters with these terrifying forces of the underworld permeate not just countries but entire, age-old cultures throughout the world. The belief in demons exists in many religions, both major and smaller in the size of their followers. Moreover, the descriptions, fears, and perceptions are largely the same in all the philosophies.

The prevalence of this idea points to many interesting conclusions, but two big potential truths come up. Namely, the fact that believers and alleged victims of demons come from all over the world can imply that demons are either real or that the idea stems from something universal—characteristic of all humans. What that could be is a broad subject, but it's certain that, as humans, we have an undeniable darkness inside us we carry from generation to generation for millennia.

Whether demons are just an irrational projection of this darkness or something real, almost tangible, and existing apart from us and at our side will probably never be confirmed beyond a reasonable doubt. But perhaps time will tell the tale, and perhaps one day, a bolt of irrefutable proof of their existence will shoot down from the sky or up from the great below and change our whole conception of reality. Until then, all we can do is listen, observe, make educated guesses, and read stories.

We can also make sure that we are protected just in case, both as a preventive measure and as a way of coping with these forces if we believe that we or someone personally close to us is being possessed. The following are a few tips on how to spot a possible demonic possession and what to do about it.

First and foremost, various behavioral changes should be looked out for. Aside from anything paranormal, which is always a sign, there may be an unseen force at work; look out for subtle and extreme shifts in behavior and attitude that have never been there before. Extreme and violent tantrums, unsettling changes in a person's voice, night terrors, unprovoked anger, regular vomiting, and other similar changes are mild signs of possession. Those who might be possessed will also usually show a powerful aversion and disgust toward anything religious or holy while developing a deep fascination with satanic and demonic matters. Extreme signs of possession would be anything supernatural or seemingly impossible that a person does. Hallucinations and strange apparitions are also always a sign to beware of.

The first step in dealing with possession is always to make sure that you aren't dealing with plain old mental illness or normal behavioral problems in a growing child. Most forms of acting up are not cause for concern about demons. If the problem is with your own self, and if you notice you are doing things that seem unbecoming of you and out of your control, then it's necessary to talk to someone like your pastor or a psychiatrist.

A common way to test for demonic possession in others is by exposing them to prayer, church, and other sanctimonious items. If there is a violent reaction, then something probably is wrong.

So, what can you do about it? For one, you can work on your spirituality and emotional strength to become more impervious. Maintaining a clean and neat environment at your home is also said to weaken demonic influence. More importantly, however, you can perform cleansing rituals helped by those who are well-versed in the matter. Remember not to underestimate these evil forces.

It's always a good idea to talk to an expert if you believe that you or anyone you know is being disturbed by demonic forces. Most regular people are less than capable of tackling a demon and there's always the possibility of making the ordeal even worse. Always talk to your local pastor or a demonologist and let them evaluate the situation and give you guidance.

Keep in mind that prevention is the best cure, as always. Maintain a wholesome life, work on your spirituality, stay in balance, and never under any circumstance challenge the forces you do not understand, as this would just be asking for trouble.

RESOURCES:

https://exemplore.com/paranormal/Do-you-know-the-difference-between-an-evil-spiritand-a-demon

https://www.youtube.com/watch?v=Djmk42Czvfg

http://www.thescarystory.com/the-exorcism-of-roland-doe/

http://coolinterestingstuff.com/the-exorcist-the-true-story-of-roland-doerobbie-mannheim

http://www.dailymail.co.uk/news/article-2449423/Devil-Roland-Doe-The-Exorcistbased-real-life-Missouri-possession.html

https://www.ranker.com/list/true-story-behind-the-exorcist/rachel-souerbry

http://mysteriousuniverse.org/2017/01/death-from-beyond-bizarre-cases-of-ouija-boardkillings/

https://www.thefreelibrary.com/Devil+worshipper+sacrificed+boy+of+15+at+DIY+altar%3B+Ouija+board+said%3A...-a061173348   https://listverse.com/2015/08/05/10-terrible-crimes-connected-to-ouija-boards/

http://www.independent.co.uk/news/ouija-killer-sent-tobroadmoor-1315300.html

https://publications.parliament.uk/pa/ld199900/ldjudgmt/jd000330/ant-1.htm

http://www.the13thfloor.tv/2016/10/10/the-ouija-board-did-it-7-real-crimes-connectedto-ouija-boards/

https://www.mirror.co.uk/news/uk-news/cruel-dog-owner-drowned-dismembered-5067252

http://www.thenorthernecho.co.uk/news/11764615.Ouija_bard_dog_killer____s_wife_and_step_daughter_arrested_after_fire_destroys_their_home/

http://www.thenorthernecho.co.uk/news/local/northdurham/stanley/11758587.Man_drowned_and_dismembered_pet_dog_after__Ouija_board_left_her_possessed_by_the_devil_/

https://www.redbookmag.com/life/news/a20173/man/

http://mysteriousuniverse.org/2015/12/demons-and-death-the-strange-case-of-michaeltaylor/

https://www.oddee.com/item_98653.aspx

https://www.youtube.com/watch?v=Gjb7qAFbPco

https://aminoapps.com/c/horror/page/blog/the-demon-murder-trial-arne-cheyenne-johnson/2vwF_Nur57kLVzElK2M7eKNbKmDdMrB

http://www.the13thfloor.tv/2016/10/18/the-demon-murder-case-of-arne-cheyennejohnson/

http://archives.law.virginia.edu/dengrove/writeup/arne-cheyenne-johnson

http://coolinterestingstuff.com/the-trial-of-arne-cheyenne-johnson

https://www.reddit.com/r/nosleep/comments/wb0ou/please_dont_actually_try_this/

https://theghostinmymachine.com/2014/02/24/the-most-dangerous-games-the-threekings/

https://www.bustle.com/p/scary-ghost-games-to-play-on-halloween-2017-at-your-ownrisk-79572

https://www.reddit.com/r/nosleep/comments/we074/i_was_the_fool/

https://www.ranker.com/list/signs-your-child-is-possessed/brandon-michaels

https://thoughtcatalog.com/anonymous/2016/12/i-played-the-elevator-game-and-i-did-it-wrong-the-woman-followed-me-back/

https://www.youtube.com/watch?v=YNBI6daZmxA

https://www.youtube.com/watch?v=TsTcYFsvxD4&feature=youtu.be

https://www.youtube.com/watch?v=VTbWSSqDr6U&t=984

https://www.youtube.com/watch?v=gC7chBqzA80

https://www.youtube.com/watch?v=7A0Kf5qD0dE

https://www.youtube.com/watch?v=ucV7NDbx5z4&feature=youtu.be

https://www.youtube.com/watch?v=8my4kfE3K2I

https://www.youtube.com/watch?v=-sbMSMdPmYg&t=271s

https://www.thoughtco.com/phantom-phone-call-stories-2593179

https://www.thoughtco.com/weird-text-messages-2595965

http://www.ghosttheory.com/2016/02/08/a-strange-death-in-vallecas-madrid

http://altereddimensions.net/2018/the-vallecas-case-the-demonic-possession-of-estefania-gutierrez-lazaro-provides-compelling-evidence-of-paranormal-activity-via-the-official-police-report-of-the-responding-officers

https://www.youtube.com/watch?v=5W9p4KyvAoU

www.ingramcontent.com/pod-product-compliance
Lightning Source LLC
Chambersburg PA
CBHW032038180726
48284CB00008B/2651